the *Misty* Effect

JOSHUA MCSWAIN

ISBN: 978-1-09839-940-5

Summer 2005

---

*H*e *had been stalking her for months.*

Grief plagued Savannah. It felt like locusts shielding the sunlight and then eating away at her until nothing was left but a dull, emotionless automaton carrying out the duties of life. For two weeks, the image would flash up: her best friend entangled in the metal clunk of what had been two cars. That would drum up the grief, then the locusts, followed by the numbness—all on repeat.

Turning the diner's sign over to "Closed," Savannah had just muddled through another grueling twelve-hour shift. Beyond exhausted, she stepped outside, into the steam bath that is the North Carolina coast. The heat was just another spice in her recipe of despair. Like every night for the past two weeks, Savannah's car essentially drove her home. She half-obeyed lights and signs until she absently turned into the condominium parking lot.

He watched her from a parked sedan. The burning light of his cigarette would give an onlooker the only indication someone was inside. But no one paid attention; anyone around was busy with their own life.

She slammed the car door, and the humid night blanketed her again. Across the street was a neighborhood ABC store that Savannah couldn't resist. She left the liquor store with a brown paper bag concealing the vodka she planned on drowning in. Keys rang their metal tune until one of them opened the door into her colorless condo. Savannah flung them onto the kitchen countertop and exhaled: she was off from work tomorrow.

Eager to get the alcohol in her system, she left the front door wide open. Orange juice filled the glass, stopping at about an inch. Vodka made up the rest. She stirred her drink and threw the spoon into the sink. Savannah gulped the mixed drink like she'd been caught in the hot desert sun all day without water.

He quietly entered the condo while Savannah was only a few feet from the door. The knife he held reflected the light along its sharp blade. David licked his lips in excitement. For years, he had wanted to murder someone. Now was his chance.

Savannah felt the sultry heat entering her condo. Her eyes found the culprit—her neglected front door. She stomped over and slammed it. Slightly bothered by her carelessness, she was too tired to let it weigh on her for more than a second. What she craved now was a long, mindless shower.

In the narrow hallway, she stripped off the stench of a hard day's work. While undressing, she continued to chug away at her strong beverage. Eager to consume the last drop of liquid and pull off her last piece of clothing, Savannah achieved both at the same time.

David admired her skin because it looked untouched. He stood behind a chest-high house plant that didn't hide him well, but he didn't care about getting caught. The upper hand belonged to him; her short, skinny form was no match for his strength. His was not the gym body most men wished to have, but a brute muscular frame a survivalist would envy. His hands could effortlessly take on any large, ravenous animal, like a wolf.

Savannah left the hall behind, and the dark bathroom came alive with light and then water. The cheap shower curtain billowed out as her elbows hit it. The plastic drapery wasn't transparent, but she could see a dark shadow moving toward her.

Her head began to swim from the stiff drink she had made, but she understood the approaching figure was no figment of her imagination nor the result of being drunk. This figure was real and present. With a stranger creeping closer and closer, hopelessness took over the space in Savannah where fear should lie.

With no fight in her, Savannah pulled back the liner and laid eyes upon the hulking intruder. She invited him, "If you're here to kill me, go ahead. I have nothing to live for." Not a single drop of fear came out of her words.

David stopped a few steps short. He didn't know what to make of her statement. She had taken away much of the thrill of killing her. He still wanted to—but less so than before.

Savannah thought back through her short life, Next month, she would be twenty-three. Already, all those who mattered to her were gone. Even her sex life was sad. She had had two awkward encounters with two different boyfriends that hadn't lasted more than a few weeks. She had prioritized other things in her life besides seeking a man.

Now, her eyes scanning this beast of a man, Savannah wanted something. By this point, the steamy mist from the shower had filled the little bathroom. She realized he had closed the door behind him. He held a long sharp knife—the blade shone.

Then she knew what she wanted, in the few minutes left to her. The words fell seductively from her lips. "But before you kill me," she asked, "can you give me something I've never had before? A climax?"

She didn't expect him to answer. Savannah watched his steely green eyes seemingly snub her request. In return, with nothing to lose, she gave David a wanton look. After a few seconds, his murderous, scorching glare subsided to a different heat. Within him, sexual energy ignited.

David barreled toward Savannah, keeping a tight grip on his knife. She shrank into the shower's dissipating steam as the spraying water grew cold. Expecting death or sex, Savannah thought either would be welcome.

David lifted Savannah, gripping her upper arms. Her nude body slapped against the cold tile. Holding onto the blade, he pressed the sharp metal side by side against her arm, creating a silver valley in her skin. He squeezed and pulled her slightly forward for a kiss, but that caused the knife to pierce the valley's edge. A red line formed. His mouth enveloped her thin lips.

The kiss was unrestrained.

She reciprocated with her tongue, finding a dance with his. The cuts continued deeper along her arm. She moaned at the pain and at the pleasure.

David felt Savannah's warm blood run down his palm. He withdrew his kiss, bordering on sloppy, removed one of his hands from Savannah, and placed the knife in his back pocket.

Blood dribbled down Savannah's arm. With callous fingers, David smeared the rosy liquid over her skin. His index finger entered her mouth.

As she tasted her blood, Savannah thrilled to the delicate dance between killer and victim. She felt more alive than ever.

She bit his finger, hard enough to bring enough pain to elicit some kind of barbaric response. Savannah wanted to be slapped or punished in some way.

Withdrawing his finger, David did just that. The forceful slap stung her face. Her eyes watered.

Both now entirely aroused, David lifted Savannah by her tiny ass and carried her to her bedroom. He threw her onto the little bed and crawled on top. His husky body pressed hers into the mattress. She didn't mind. She felt like she was being hugged. She wanted desperately to be wanted—even if it was from a murderous stranger, and even if his desire was fleeting.

Missionary sex proceeded, first in a dying-of-hunger way, finally in a being-fed way. Both wanted it so badly that all grace went out the window. Only savagery twisted the bedsheets beneath them. Both achieved orgasm in a wet clash that left the nerves in their legs twitching. David stayed inside her until she fell asleep, which was less than a minute. The combination of booze and sex conked her out.

Savannah didn't dream.

Savannah awoke in David's embrace. The morning sunlight cut through the blinds and streaked in ribbons across her bedroom. Her head pounded. The events of the night before came into focus. Last night, she'd had sex with a man who'd planned to kill her. Savannah lay in bed in a frozen panic, controlling her breathing. She wanted to fly out of the room and away from this man. Contrary to her resignation last night, she no longer wanted to die. She wanted to live.

How to get out of this situation? Savannah posed the question in her mind. She remembered the knife the man had, cringing at the thought that he could stab her at any moment. *Maybe he's just waiting for me to wake up before he kills me,* Savannah guessed. With her nervous system pulsing, she acted by rolling carefully onto her side to face him.

His eyes were wide open, like he'd been waiting hours for her to rise.

Savannah forced a smile. "Good morning. Last night was fun," she could detect a hint of fakery in her voice.

So could David.

She instantly recognized that he still wanted to kill her.

Savannah leaped off the bed and landed in front of the sliding glass door to her patio. She flung it open and thrust herself out, slamming the door behind her and screaming into the parking lot.

"Helllllllp!!!" With no way to lock it from the outside, she held the door handle closed. The patio was screened, offering her no quick escape. She would have to tear through the screen.

A neighbor was headed to his car when her scream stopped him in his tracks. The young man spun around to face Savannah, standing a few feet away from her patio. Their eyes met. "How can I help?"

"A man is about to kill me," Savannah said, breathless in her desperation. "He's inside my condo!"

The sliding door began to tug back from her grip.

Through the glass she saw David pulling. Savannah pushed in on the door and wailed for her neighbor to help. "Please help me! He's trying to stab me!!" She spotted the large knife he held as he jerked the door open. Savannah fell back and hit the floor.

David stepped confidently onto the patio.

She scrambled back up and her nails clawed into the screen. Her tiny fist punched a hole into the mesh. Using the gap, she ripped the screen outward and threw her body into it.

The neighbor stepped up to the porch and seized Savannah's hand while her body dangled halfway out. He saw David approach her with the knife and yelled, "Leave her alone! What are you doing? You won't get away with this!" The neighbor tried frantically to pull Savannah out, but her body was caught in a tangled web of torn wires.

David stabbed Savannah's lower back.

Defeated and short of breath, she whimpered, "Hel—p."

Using the knife as leverage, David pulled her into the patio and flung her against the condo's outside wall.

She crashed onto the floor, knocking her breath out. She tried to roll herself upright, but the pain paralyzed her. She moaned a plea to David, "Please don't."

Blatantly ignoring her, David bent over, held up the knife, and began what would be multiple stabbings.

The neighbor reached into his pocket for his flip phone. His hands shaking from what he was witnessing, he could barely dial the numbers 911.

Savannah passed out from the wrenching pain of the third stab. She dreamed of running in a forest; a woman came into view. Savannah stopped and knew instantly: this was not a dream, but rather death.

CHAPTER 1
The Preacher

Breathless from a morning of sex, I rolled off Saris and wrapped my body in the cool sheets.

He unfurled my cotton cocoon and leaned in, giving me a vigorous kiss. His strong hands caressed up my thighs, leaving behind a trail of arousing chill bumps. He pulled back and gave me a look, intimating he wanted to go again.

I reminded him he had to be at the church to set up for tomorrow's sermon. "You got a lot to do."

His church had just undergone repairs and a light remodeling, and needed to be cleaned up before tomorrow.

"I know, but you're what I *want* to do."

I laughed off his cheesy line.

Saris sighed and rolled away from me. He stood up by the edge of the bed, nude, displaying a body you wouldn't expect from a preacher. The hair on his chest and abdomen did little to hide his pecs and chiseled abs. His legs held him up well, and with the slightest distribution of his weight, the calves would flex their muscle. The hair on his legs couldn't hide their mountain-climber strength. A good body is nice. However, I'm more of a face person, and he hits all the right qualifications: eyes and expressions that don't appear dubious but instead loving. At forty-five, he maintained a boyish complexion along with eyes filled with wisdom. His face carried an old-world authority that would make most people follow him at any point in time. I could hear the naysayers judge: that determining someone's personality by their face, mannerisms, and tics seems like a psychic reading someone's palm.

I think there's a science for spotting questionable individuals. Think about it: for millennia, we needed to know if we could trust someone, either to collaborate or to copulate. Otherwise, they would steal from us or even kill us if necessary. Everyone gives off subtle facial clues about their intent, though they're usually hidden behind a fake expression. When we can't recognize the signs of someone's nature, that puts us at a disadvantage for survival. Evolution has taught us, subconsciously and consciously, how to spot a bad person—if you look and listen carefully enough. I think that skill is fading in this modern era, though. Because, thankfully, we're not living in barbaric times.

At least, so it seems.

Anyway, his eyes were blue, but the color never really mattered to me. Even as he stood there, those blue eyes were still giving me a piercing plea to go one more time.

I was tempted by his wordless offer, but I knew the long day he had in store. Also, his stamina that morning had left me tired out. With those rationalizations, I gave him the "No" look.

He sulked away with a childish frown and began to dress.

I stumbled out of bed, barely able to walk due to my morning exertions and, begrudgingly, began to get ready as well.

The mirror revealed a slightly overweight woman, something I've been most of my life. I still remember the seemingly helpful—but always hurtful—comments from various people in my past.

"Misty, you would look so sexy or beautiful if you would just lose a few pounds," would be followed by, "You have such a beautiful face." At forty-two years old, I don't think I will ever have a slim and toned body, nor do I have the mental energy or time to be that vain anymore. I do, however, appreciate my still youthful look, blue eyes, and natural red hair.

I looked over at Saris dressing. I wondered if he could look into my eyes and see that I harbor a cold side. My nature hasn't always been good. I exhibited terrible behavior in the past, especially when it came to my ex-husband. I sensed that Saris knew I had a suspect history, but he still made me feel loved and wanted. In appreciation of that feeling, I turned to him and said, "We do need to shower—don't we?"

He grinned back delightfully and replied, "We are dirty." His raspy bass voice vibrated through me, arousing me with a tingling sensation that raised my skin, setting me adrift and warming my body. His eyes dipped, motioning to the shower. The bathroom opened directly off the bedroom, and it was as if the room was luring us. I reversed my dressing, undoing buttons and unzipping my pants. My clothes dropped at my feet.

Saris stripped, in sort of a funny dance.

I started to giggle, but my lips froze. I needed him to ravage me. My want had become a must—no time for games.

He recognized the seriousness of my desire and abruptly stopped his playful dancing. He kicked his jeans off, leaving him naked again.

I inhaled excitedly at his flushed muscular body and tossed black hair. His blue eyes examined my body, foreshadowing naughty things to come. He turned toward the bathroom, showing me his rippled backside. Mesmerized by every part of him, I followed him, my thoughts a blank.

In the shower, Saris seized my hips and pulled me fervently against himself. About a foot taller than me, he had an alpha presence that melted every pillar of strength I might hold against him. His hands glided up from my lower back, and I trembled from the trail of delight on my skin. I stepped back, allowing my buttocks to hit the shower knob. The warm water sprayed out onto us while he lifted my chin and planted a deep sensual kiss. The kiss traveled to my neck, unleashing stimulation with each brush of his tongue. My body went limp, giving up all control. Without any effort, he lifted me onto him—and entered me.

I let out a euphoric moan and clenched all of him.

And the rhythm started, the pace slow at first, but tracks were laid toward a finish line. Saris's irresistible maleness along with his rhythm set me aloft and hurtling toward that finish line. And, at last, I crossed.

Once dressed, we made our way to the kitchen and brewed a quick cup of coffee. We sat at the kitchen island in comfortable silence for a bit, checking our phones. Saris sat up straight, reminding me once again how his six feet, five inches towered over me. I turned off my phone and placed it in the kitchen drawer, determined to stay unplugged for the day. That was easy for me to do.

Like a puppy, I followed Saris to the door for a goodbye kiss.

He opened the door and the morning sun revealed the gray hiding in his short, wavy black hair. Saris Carlyle, the preacher, turned and spoke with that gorgeous baritone voice. "Goodbye, babe. You enjoy your day off," he said with a warm smile.

I responded blissfully, "You, too," standing on my toes for a kiss.

He leaned in, and we kissed, not in passing, but with a purpose that wasn't forced or contrived. It was a show of true love—something I never thought I would have at this point in my life.

Reluctantly, I pulled away from his warm lips and waved him off. As I watched him walk to his Jeep, I realized I was torn this morning. I both didn't want him to go, and I did. I both enjoyed his presence and warmth and also didn't mind having the house to myself for the day. I wanted to catch up on some me time. I was thinking all this while watching his car pull out of the driveway and disappear up the forested road.

The sun was pouring over the trees on this bright spring morning. Deeply inhaling the fresh, dewy air, I closed and locked the door behind me. A yearning to bring that air inside inspired my next move.

I walked around the house opening windows to let in the crisp—but not cold—breeze. It combined with the new-lumber smell that permeated the home, all adding up to a relaxing aroma.

This two-story house had been built nearly a year ago. It sat at the end of a cul-de-sac in a new development. The street had only one other house. The rest was wooded lots parceled off by ribbons and for-sale signs, but development had slowed to a halt. With only two occupied residences, the vast neighborhood had a serene quiet. Nature remained a dominant force. It was nothing to see several deer in the road, a red fox or even a black bear.

While opening the last window on the second floor, I realized I loved the house's large, double-panel windows. Raising those sashes seemed old-fashioned. It took heavy lifting; there was no remote. I was surprised the builder hadn't offered an automated window. However, I didn't mind the chore; it gave me a little exercise. I had an affinity for doing things like in a bygone era. I was one of those people who used a typewriter while listening to vinyl records.

I did love the house's colors and modern look. Throughout, meticulous white trim and massive doors set off varying shades of light blue on the walls. Thick crown molding accented the high ceilings in almost every room. Laminated floors in shades of gray glistened against neatly outlined white baseboards. Patterned occasional rugs dotted the shiny wood, and the stairs were carpeted in royal blue and lined with a glossy white balustrade topped with a thin railing, painted in the same blue. Hints of yellow and brown also dotted the décor around the house.

Gliding down the stairs, I turned to face a bookcase built into the side wall. I grabbed a book I'd wanted to delve into and made my way to the kitchen. A bay window offered a view of the large backyard and pool, already shimmering in the morning sun slicing through the trees from the eastern horizon. Freshly cut grass gave way to a deep forest that bordered the lot. I rested against the oversized pillows on the window seat, I ran my hands against the book's cool cover and inhaled slowly. I closed my eyes briefly and reflected on how happy I was. Maybe it was the morning sex, but I was also at peace. A tranquility that had been long fought for. With that thought, I opened the book and started to get lost in someone else's narrative.

Chapter 2

The Intruder

---

*U*nknown to Misty, a man stood under the trees that bordered the lot. He peered out of the shadowed forest like a predator. Steadily, he watched Misty peacefully settle into the bay window with her book. Had anyone seen him, his eyes and expression would have betrayed his agenda, which concluded with a bad outcome for anyone who came across his path. He stood about six feet tall with a muscular, stocky build. His green eyes emitted a cold intensity against a pale face. When the time came to make his move, he stepped out of the woods unnoticed. He followed the neighboring lot's tree line, entered the empty street, and walked to the front door. He grabbed the doorknob and slowly turned. Inside, the house was mostly silent; the faint sound of the doorknob turning didn't travel to the kitchen where Misty read quietly. As he pulled on the door, he immediately realized she had locked it. He quickly shifted to another plan to gain entrance.

I sat up in the bay window with a realization the coffee was beckoning me to the bathroom. Still in socks, I gleefully skated through the kitchen and braked just short of the dining area. A short hallway connected the two rooms to the bathroom. I entered. It felt invigoratingly cool; its half-opened window freshened the room with early spring air and acted as a speaker for the chirping birds outside.

Sitting on the toilet's cold rim jolted me a little and awakened a sense that something wasn't right. All at once, the birds had flown away, taking their comforting melodies with them. I scanned the dead silent room, and my eyes became fixed on the shower curtain in front of me. A slight ripple in the green fabric set my heart racing. Was someone or something back there? I wondered.

I felt a presence lurking nearby. I glanced out the window and saw no sign of a breeze; I felt nothing blowing into the room. The air was still, with no fans or central AC going. For some reason, that put my mind in a near panic. An urge came over me: I had to solve the mystery of what lay behind the shower curtain.

Hurriedly finished with relieving myself, I shot up from the toilet, zipping my pants. I paced the few steps to the shower. The curtain rippled to a stop. Apprehension devoured me and revved up my heart into fast, loud thumping in my ears. Leaning in slightly, I snatched back the shower curtain, revealing nothing but paranoia. I unclenched and exhaled, releasing the tension, softly laughing at my unwarranted fear. Realizing it was myself entering the bathroom and the door's motion that caused the shower curtain to move, I turned to leave. But something caught the corner of my eye.

Something moved.

My paranoia vanished, replaced with truth. A human hand placed itself on the windowsill. Fast-rising adrenaline pulsed throughout my body, a pure fright I'd never experienced before. Ever.

My reaction was swift and quick; I reached over and slammed the window down onto the intruder's hand. He stepped into view from the window; I stood there screaming, maintaining my hold on the window pressing into his flesh, keeping his hand locked in. Afraid to look directly at him, I registered that he was stocky and pale, and taller than me. I thought I knew him.

Before I could make out any more details of the intruder's appearance, I realized his other hand was free. I abandoned my hold on the window and leaped out of the bathroom. I slammed the door shut behind me to slow down any possible chase. At the front door, I stopped with the realization that it was a short distance from the bathroom window. Even if I made it out, I had no car to get into, and the nearest neighbor was a long way up the street. It hit me: I was trapped in the house.

I hesitated in the living room at the foot of the stairs, contemplating my next move. Rocking my body, I was ready to run. I kept my eyes on the bathroom door, while listening for any sounds that came out. I realized my phone was in the kitchen. *I can call 911.* But as I turned to get my phone, I could hear footsteps charging full speed behind me. I pivoted and fled, knowing I couldn't make it out the front door in time; after wasting precious seconds unlocking it, I would no doubt be in this intruder's deadly hands. Instead, I bolted up the stairs.

How in the hell did he get in from the kitchen? I wondered. I hadn't even opened any windows on that side of the house. I abandoned the inquiry and focused on my run to safety. I felt him close behind, my back arched in anticipation of a bullet or a weapon. I ducked into the upstairs bathroom because it's right off the stairs, and I could lock myself in.

I slammed the door so quickly I couldn't remember if I locked it. I doubled checked my efforts with a stare at the latch. *It's horizontal, it's locked. It's horizontal, it's locked,* I told myself a few times. With my eyes fixed on the door, I backed toward the bathroom's only window though I knew I couldn't escape that way without taking a massive fall. The window was high, with nothing between it and the ground.

I began to look around for a weapon, then heard—and saw—the lock turn. In a mere second, I remembered that a key had rested at the top of the door ledge—on the outside. *Damn.* The key was there in case anybody got locked out of the bathroom. Nobody had ever thought you would need to barricade yourself in a bathroom. The door opened.

In a panic, I grabbed the large mirror, ripped it off the wall, and flung it towards the intruder. His arm deflected the mirror and a cascade of shattering glass exploded across the floor. I scrambled into the shower behind me and slammed shut the sliding door. The force of the slam caused the shower glass to crack but not give way.

With a death grip on the metal handle, I watched the man weaving as if slightly stunned as he shook off some glass. With some relief, I realized I didn't see a weapon. *Maybe I knocked it out of his hand.* I probed the floor, finding nothing resembling a weapon. *Is he here to rape me?* I watched in horror as he resumed his way towards me. Then I felt it in my gut: *He's about to kill me with his bare hands.*

That's when I thought about my deceased daughter. She, too, had been strangled. *No! This can't be happening.* I started to scream but stopped, realizing it would be pointless as there were no neighbors to hear. My only hope seemed to be reasoning with the intruder.

"Take what you want. I don't care. I won't report you. Just leave." When that got no response, I began to lie desperately.

"I have a thirteen-year-old daughter, and she needs me. Please don't hurt me." Suppressing my tears, I continued to lie. "My husband is on his way back. He went to get me breakfast. You better leave before he gets here. Wait! I think I hear him downstairs," I said in my most convincing tone.

That last statement made the intruder pause. His hand stopped inches from the shower door's outside handle. Suddenly I knew. I needed to seize this pause. Summoning up my fight response, I flung open the door, hitting him with every ounce of force I had. The glass door shattered, once again bombarding the intruder with glass.

I hoped he was stunned enough as I scrambled around him. I'd gotten only a few steps when suddenly I felt my left wrist clamped into an unbreakable grip. My dream of getting away, utterly dashed.

He spun me to face him. I had time to register the fury and some small cuts on his face before I tucked down my head and charged at him. I used my body and free hand to push him back into the shower, hoping to trip him on the shower door's remnants. He responded with his firm grip, twisting my wrist over my head while forcing my body back. With his other hand, he pushed against my stomach, blocking my charge.

I changed tactics. I tried to free my hand by pulling backward away from him. I positioned myself toward the bathroom door, ready to dart out if, miraculously, he lost his grip. All this was at great peril of my wrist. I could see my hand turning blue but felt only a dull pain. I knew adrenaline was keeping the full force of pain at bay.

He yanked me in aggressively toward him, his strength overpowering mine as he grabbed my other hand. With both of his hands occupied, gripping my wrists, I started to kick at him hysterically and I bit down on his fist. He forcefully twisted his hand out of my teeth, keeping control of my hands. My effort to break free felt futile, but I knew I couldn't give up, so I frantically jerked about, trying to wrestle free. Shoving both wrists, he painfully slammed me into a corner.

Literally cornered, I cried out. "What do you want from me?"

I sensed he was trying to make eye contact, but I couldn't bring myself to look at him. I wanted to keep my neck down for fear of him choking me. Then I heard his voice.

"I'm here to kill you. Isn't it obvious?" His tone was cruel and joking; his voice was deep and frightening. I felt he had done this many times before.

In my frantic state, I barely noticed the toilet but quickly seized an idea. Placing a foot on the lid, I propelled myself up, with enough momentum to wrap my legs around his waist. The unexpected force of my weight made him stumble back.

To regain control, he let go of my right wrist. Feeling the intruder pushing at my legs wrapped around his waist, I began to punch at his hand. I could feel myself losing my balance, so I stopped punching and clenched his hair. I now hovered back and forth over his head. That threw him into a frenzy, trying to push me off. With my only free hand, I tightened my grip on his hair at the back of his head. That let me hold on, staving off his efforts to get the upper hand again.

He hurled a clenched fist in my direction. I jerked my head to avoid his punch. He followed his failed blow with a ripping grip on my hair, pulling my head back. That left me facing the ceiling and forced me to unlatch my grip on his hair. Desperately grasping for something, I found his ear, wrapped my hand around it and pulled with all my might. The intruder growled and our bodies spun around the cramped space. I sensed he was losing his footing, about to fall, when we slammed sideways into the door, cracking it. The hit helped him steady himself somewhat.

At the door, he pulled my head back even more forcefully. I dug my nails into his ear to get more traction, making him snarl and pull at my fingers, trying to break my grip. Confident I had found a weakness, I clenched and pulled harder. The intruder emitted a deep, short cry of pain. His hand shifted its focus back to my legs, still wrapped around his waist. While his fingers attempted to tear into my thighs, I wiggled my legs, tightening their grasp around his waist. I threw my body backward, making him stumble, but his free hand smacked the wall, letting him keep his balance. I knew I couldn't relent. I needed to keep my hold on this man. If I gave up, I knew, that would mean death for me.

Our scuffle paused for an instant; he appeared to be catching his breath or thinking. My legs started to shake, weakening their hold. Suddenly, he pulled my hair harder than before, jerking my head farther back. A stinging pain spread across my skull. I kept my legs' precarious grip on his body, but I now faced upside down. Adrenaline no longer subdued the pain, now spreading from my scalp to my face. I wished my hair would give way, relieving some of the agonizing force. Tears welled up, barely allowing me to see we were just outside the bathroom, a few feet away from the stairs. I already felt death was imminent, but I knew to fight with every breath. I knew then that I needed to get us to tumble down these stairs, even if it killed me in the process.

The scuffle picked up again as I dug my feet into the bow of his back to move us closer to the stairs. I also used my tight grip on his ear as leverage. Inch by inch, we were getting closer to the stairs, and then I felt a rip. A warm liquid dotted my arms, followed by something oozing over my hand.

He yelled, "Ahhh! Fucking bitch!"

I assumed I had ripped his ear. But what I guessed was blood oozing onto my fingers made it difficult to hang on.

Once I lost my grasp on his ear, I threw myself back in a roll, my legs still wrapped around him. He crashed against me and released my hair. An instant of relief on my head gave way to a painful blow to my back when I slammed onto the stairwell, making it difficult to move.

In acute pain, I lay sprawled on the top three steps with the intruder's weight on top of me. An attempt to throw us down the stairs failed. I tried to decide my next move, but my legs were on the wrong side of his body to kick him in the groin.

He lifted himself off me, but the pain in my back prevented me from raising myself quickly, especially from my awkward angle on the stairs. Before I could raise my arms to fight, I could feel his bloodied hands grab them again.

He lifted me and laid me on the floor at the top of the stairs. The move made the pain shoot through me, making me jerk slightly. That twitch spooked the intruder into thinking I had more fight in me. He hurriedly locked in my legs together between his knees and clasped one hand around my weakened wrists. Hovering over me, he exhaled triumphantly.

Flat on my back awaiting my fate, I wanted to take a good look at the man who was about to kill me. I took some satisfaction to see the ear was, in fact, ripped and covered in blood, in addition to the cuts on his face. At least I had fought back, I thought. Throughout our fight, I had never gotten a good look at his face or into his eyes. When I did so, silently pleading for my life, it suddenly hit me. I gasped in recognition. I did indeed know this man. I just couldn't believe it was him.

I had once hired him to kill a man.

CHAPTER 3
Awaiting Fate

Seeing that I recognized him, he spoke with a cold smirk. "Hello, Misty. How are you doing these days?"

I locked eyes on him.

"Hello, David," I said, more weakly than I'd intended. Louder, but my voice still scratchy, I asked, "Who hired you?"

Still smirking, he placed his free hand on my throat. In fearful anticipation that it might be my last, I took a deep breath.

With his hand just resting there, he answered the question. "Why, your ex-husband did. He wanted me to choke you. You know: the same way your daughter died."

A sudden rush overwhelmed my body. I started to feel hot; anger brewed and erupted. I rose, no longer in pain, swung my arm and in a fury pushed this man down the stairs. I watched him tumble into the banister near the bottom, shattering the wood and breaking his fall.

Crouching at the top of the stairs, breathing hard, I let my anger bubble over and condense into a plan. *I'm going to kill this fucker. And I'm going to kill Tyler.* Tyler was my ex-husband, and a year ago I had chickened out. *That was a mistake.* I'd called it off just minutes before David—most likely a fake name—had been scheduled to kill Tyler.

I remembered the remorseful call I had made to this hired hit man. We had established a "safe word" to use in case I changed my mind. It was an easy and self-explanatory word. Over the phone, I'd kept saying, "*Stop, stop, stop.*"

It had taken several seconds for him to respond, and he answered back with only one word. "OK."

I had decided to leave Tyler instead of having him killed. Up to that moment, I had never thought leaving him was an option; not one that would leave me alive. I'd feared the man then and I still did.

It was no surprise that Tyler still blamed me for my daughter's death three years ago. Her name was Lily, after my grandmother. He attributed our thirteen-year-old daughter's kidnapping and murder to my absence, as a working mom. Many times he said, "You should have been home when she came home from school that day."

It was shortly after Lily's death when the physiological torture and the beatings began. I did very little to fight back because, at first, I thought I deserved it. I blamed myself for her death, too. Anyway, it was hard even to imagine standing up to Tyler. He was a powerful man, rich from real estate in his twenties, and now a respected police officer.

After Lily died, I sold my business for next to nothing. The diner had been successful, but I couldn't work from the grief. That was a mistake. Once the money dried up, I became dependent on Tyler. Towards the end of our marriage, I felt trapped financially and then physically by his ever-increasing threats if I left him. Caged into a life with Tyler, I thought a hit man was the only key to freeing myself.

A day after backing out of my arrangement with David, I worked up my courage and filed for divorce. But to this day, I never understood why Tyler wanted me to stay married to him, given that he held such hatred for me. It wasn't about money; we had a prenup, so a divorce wouldn't threaten any of his assets. And it wasn't about sex, since after Lily died, we didn't do that.

A few days after my aborted attempt to have Tyler killed, I met Saris. Saris saved my life. He ignited new hope inside me. I was on the verge, being self-destructive. I wouldn't say suicidal, because a small part of me did want to live. That part wanted to see justice for my daughter's murder. Once I shared my story—and my guilt— with Saris, he gave me a new perspective. And just in time. My daughter's killer was caught and sentenced to death shortly after my blossoming friendship with Saris began. Once that bitter chapter had closed, Saris gave me a reason to live.

It was only a few months later that our friendship turned into romance. After a good night of shared thoughts, he'd leaned in for a kiss. That kiss revealed an innermost yearning that had lain subconsciously in both of us for months. That night, we gave into desire and ever since have been inseparable. Most important, after that night, I still had a friend to confide in. Going through all this from the top of the stairs, I realized the warmth and safety of my relationship with Saris had caused me to let down my guard. My fear of Tyler had subsided.

Amid all these reflections on the past, I kept my eyes on David, the intruder. He had verified my suspicions. *He's here to choke me to death.* When I'd hired him to kill Tyler, I hadn't given him specifics on how I wanted it done. I just wanted it done. *I wish I had gone through with it.*

I watched David slowly stumble back up from the broken stair rail. I realized I couldn't call the police; because Tyler *is* the police. However, now I was less afraid and more determined. I knew then that I needed to kill this man, that I couldn't let him leave this house. But first, I had questions.

David finally got his balance and positioned himself to charge back up the stairs.

Boldly, I yelled, "Come at me, fucker. I will kick your ass right back down those stairs!" I could tell he had been weakened, his ear was still bleeding, and he was turning white. "I don't think you could take another fall, so come on!" Realizing that this warning might inadvertently provoke him, I softened my voice. "Did Tyler come to you?"

He stopped to answer the question. "No. I came to him. After what you told me, I thought maybe he would have a reason to kill his wife. It wasn't hard to get Tyler to hire me after I told him you hired me to kill him. I told him you backed out, last minute. And that I kept the thirty thousand dollar deposit anyway."

I remembered, *That was the last of my hard-earned savings.*

"Well, that was just a few nails in your coffin, sweetheart." He paused, maybe to think or maybe just to catch his breath. "Anyway, that was a year ago when you hired me. I've had no clients since then, and I need the money. So I sought out a potential client. I got to eat like everyone else." Another pause gave him new vigor. "He's paying double," he bragged, "with a sixty-grand deposit and another sixty when the job is done. Look at it this way, darling, once I choke the life out of you, I won't have to kill again for a year." Finishing his statement with a devious smile, he began to climb the stairs, slow and casual, as if he was taunting me.

I had an idea from our earlier struggle, a feeling this would work. I ran back into the bathroom and there it was. I had wanted to do this earlier. I lifted the heavy lid off the toilet tank. By the time I turned around, David was at the door awaiting his fate.

We both charged at each other, and we met midway in the room as I slammed the porcelain tank lid into his shoulder. The force threw his body into the glass shower door, the panel that hadn't broken yet. Sturdy as the glass was, the impact was strong enough to crack it. I dropped the toilet tank cover and successfully made my way around him this time. I fled the bathroom with a clear understanding: somehow, I had to kill him and dispose of the body.

Glancing down the stairs, I saw the loose post broken in his fall. I hurried down and began to pull at the fractured wood with a plan to stab him with it. I could hear him coming out of the bathroom, cursing under his breath. Using my foot as leverage, I twisted at the post, leaving splinters in my hand.

I heard his feet on the steps behind me and sped up my efforts, making my hands bleed as I struggled. With seconds and inches to spare, I pulled out a perfectly jagged length of wood and started stabbing at him. He successfully dodged each of my thrusts, then caught one stab with his hand, immediately drawing blood. That's when I took the punch.

CHAPTER 4

Fifteen Minutes to Death

Dizzied from the punch, I stumbled down the last step and backward into the living room. My legs hit an end table where a small gray stone statue rests. I picked it up. It's the figure of a man with the earth on his shoulders, using both hands to hold the world. It's called Atlas, from the Greek myth. I held it over my head as David approached, a little swagger in his step despite the blood all over him. Seeing the sculpture in my hand, he stopped and said, "Come on, Misty. This is pointless. Before this morning is over you'll be dead." Glancing at the clock, he sharpened his threat. "You'll be dead before 10 a.m."

I saw that the clock showed 9:45. "You're the one that's fifteen minutes to death."

With a grimace, he snatched up a table lamp, yanking its plug from the socket, and flung it in my direction. Trying to dodge it, I fell backward onto the sofa, knocking it over, causing me to roll out the other side. Losing my hold on the statue, Atlas broke on the floor. Before I could get up, he forced me back down.

Now under him, I began kicking and screaming, but I started to believe what he had just said. *It is pointless.* He had me pinned down with his hands and legs, then he firmly clutched my throat. Suddenly, I couldn't breathe. *Fight,* I commanded myself. That thought led me to realize I had a hand free. So I began to grab at his eyes. He lost his focus, then his grip on my throat, for just a second. I gasped the precious air.

He regained his hold on my throat, more tightly this time. Now my vision got blurry, though I could still make out his devilish glare. Almost subconsciously, I realized my hand was grasping for something, and then I felt it. The remains of the statue were in my hand. I got a firm grip and swung the figure into what I thought was David's head. With the momentum of my swing, I felt its weight lighten, and heard a loud grunt. Once I felt the statue had made a solid impact, I let go. I could barely see what was going on. I could feel his grip on my throat weakening.

His grasp loosened and I choked for air, narrowly pinpointing David's hovering silhouette through my fuzzy vision. Droplets fell on my chest; his hand's pressure eased and finally vanished from my throat. Then came a rumbling thud, right beside me. I thought I had knocked him unconscious, maybe even killed him, but couldn't be sure. With a few more gasps, my nostrils vacuumed up oxygen, pulling me back from death's door.

My vision slowly cleared up, revealing that I had successfully stabbed David with Atlas. The figure's hands, which a few minutes ago had held up the world, now thrust solidly into the side of David's head. Over in the corner lay the earth. Atlas had let go of the world to save my life. Silently, I thanked the inanimate Greek hero. Keeping my fingers crossed, I couldn't tell if David was lying unconscious—or dead. I staggered to my feet and began to kick at him. No response. His eyes remained closed with no sign of flinching.

I bent over slightly and pushed the statue deeper into his head. The figure's right hand pierced David's temple, near the eye. Blood bubbling from this wound began to pour over his face and hair. Still no response. Watching this cascade of blood for a few seconds, I began to feel more confident that he was dead.

Ripping the statue out of his skull caused a greater tsunami of red to stream across the laminated floors. I grabbed a blanket off the sofa and used it to stop the blood jetting from his head. The yellow fleece soaked up his essence and adhered to his face. I spread out the remaining fabric and rolled him into it. He jutted out from the knees down, but that was OK. Because everything else wasn't OK.

I stood over him, pondering where I was going to put him. As I contemplated this, I looked at the clock. It was 9:50 a.m.

"More like five minutes to death," I said quietly to him, wrapped in my favorite blanket. That got me looking at the first-floor bathroom where it all started. I began to drag the body across the smooth floor toward the bathroom. My wrist and back announced their pain, but that didn't slow me down. I just knew I needed to get him in the shower.

Finally, out of breath from the dead weight of a man I had just killed, I stood over him in the shower. I turned the water on to wash the blood off me while he lay at my feet. Maybe it was the shock of it all, but I didn't care that I was standing over a dead man. The warm water made my clothes stick to my skin, so I began to undress and look at my wounds. My wrist emitted a stinging pain and was significantly bruised. Strands of my hair came out onto my hand from when he pulled so tightly.

Reality began to seep in, and then I realized what I was up against. How was I going to explain this to Saris? Would he understand? Of course, I never told him I had put a hit out on Tyler. I had told him everything else but that. I could never bring up the fact that I'd tried to have my ex-husband killed. Saris had a very understanding nature, but I didn't think he would understand that. He knew about my daughter; he knew Tyler had beaten and controlled me. When I realized my ex-husband was still out there with a death wish on me, I began to hyperventilate.

The shower started to get cold, and slowly I began to calm myself. In my chaos, I began to focus my mind on one thought at a time. First things first: I had to get rid of this body. Then I figured out how.

I turned the shower off and leaned my head against the wall, resting for a moment before I resumed my morning from hell. As the seconds passed, I watched the water drip from my nude body, forming trails that ran under the lifeless man. My blood-stained clothes draped over his body had turned a deep pink.

Lifting my head, I stepped out, grabbed a towel and quickly dried myself. I left the bathroom to put on a change of clothes, lace my sneakers, then raced back. Irrationally, I feared the man would somehow be moved or rise from the dead while I was gone. I was relieved to see he still lay dead in the shower.

I unwound the fleece wrapped around him and began the process of undressing the body—David, as he called himself. To keep from looking at him, his dead pale nakedness, I zoned out and had flashbacks to when Tyler would beat me.

Tyler is tall, not as tall as Saris, but more physically fit. He is also dangerously intuitive. He commands respect when he enters a room. He has a look of discipline. His brown hair is always short and perfectly cut. I've rarely seen him with a beard or a five o' clock shadow. His brown eyes emit an intelligence and a wit that the average person wouldn't want to challenge. His high cheekbones and clean-cut good looks keep the women around him blind to his faults. It is that, combined with his domineering presence, that make the women around him overtly attracted to him.

In the first fifteen years of our marriage, before our daughter died, Tyler had only slapped me one time. I chalked it up as a fluke. But by a few months after Lily died, he would punch and slap me just about every week. I would fight back on some occasions, but it would be pointless because he was much stronger than I am. Not to mention that, deep down, I felt I deserved it in some way. I figured I was rightfully being punished for not being home the day Lily was abducted and killed.

Eventually, though, I tried to fix my mind on how to get back at him. I just knew I had to kill him, but I didn't know how. Getting away with it would prove difficult, especially given the fact he is a respected police officer. The investigation into his death would be more meticulous. That would be the case for any officer's death. I couldn't choke him, I knew. He would overpower me in a second. If he had been the one who came in to kill me today instead of David, I knew I would be dead by now.

I started to regain focus on the chore in front of me. The hired killer lay completely nude. Again, I didn't allow my eyes to rest on him for more than one second. I gathered David's wet clothes and the fleece and placed them in a heap on the floor beside me. In the cabinet under the sink, I grabbed two bath towels and patted one all over his body, and I used the other to rake the shower walls and floor of water.

Once I thought he and the shower were dry enough, I left the bathroom again, feeling less fearful. In the garage, I grabbed the gas can, and to my relief, found it half full. On the way back, I stopped at the kitchen and found a lighter. With gas and lighter in hand, I stood at the bathroom door. I paused at what I was about to do. With a deep, reluctant sigh, I proceeded. I turned on the ventilation fan and fully opened the window I'd slammed onto his hand—the window where it all started.

The shower was fully lined with smooth, dark stone. I thought this was a perfect place to disappear a man in a slow burn. I ripped down the flammable shower curtain and liner, draping the polyester and plastic over him. The shower provided me enough room to maneuver around. I poured a few small lines of gasoline on him. With lighter in hand, I ignited the liner near his face. I kept the flame away from the gas for a moment. I didn't want a sudden rush of fire. I stepped back and watched the flame as it slowly burned its way to the lines of gas. I was, for some reason expecting a jolt from him but there was no movement.

Once the gasoline-doused part caught, thick black smoke immediately swamped me and the room. I pulled my shirt over my nose, and I quickly rectified the situation by turning the shower on, bringing the blaze to a sizzling halt. *OK*, I thought, *this is not the way to dispose of this body. Too much smoke. I'm back at square one.*

I felt a little stupid for thinking this would work, but I forgave myself due to my mental circumstances. I rested on the toilet seat. Feeling defeated, I zoned out for an indeterminate period. A small bloodstain on the windowsill broke my spell. David's blood brought me back to my war with Tyler. From the depths of my guts, a new fear churned inside me.

Is Tyler watching? I wondered. With that dreadful question lingering, I sat up and looked fully out the bathroom window. I didn't see or notice anything out of the ordinary. The shadowed woods around the house offered plenty of hiding spots. Paranoid, I closed the window. I decided to leave David in the shower as I made my way out of the bathroom. I needed to see if Tyler was watching before I disposed of David differently.

Outside the bathroom, I looked across the silent house, which revealed the battle for my life: the broken stair railing, an upturned couch, and a bloodied statue. If Saris came home now, I would have some explaining to do. I decided I would tell a partial lie and say an intruder had tried to kill me. I would leave out his ties to me and my ex-husband, Tyler.

An eerie calm lingered. The house seemed to relax after the insidious acts it had witnessed. Blood dotted the place from behind the upturned couch to the top of the stairs. The bold red stood out against grey floors and white carpets. I realized red was a color that hadn't inhabited this space until now. Looking at this scene, I felt my battle had just begun. I also couldn't shake the sense that I was being watched.

To quell that fear, I had to go outside. I felt a sudden urge to get out of this house. It was a feeling of being trapped inside that moved me. I unlocked the front door with a thought: locking this door had done little to protect me. Then I realized I had left the kitchen door unlocked. That's how David had gotten in.

I opened the front door to reveal a warm, sunny spring day. Inhaling the fresh air, I made my way to the street. The atmosphere brought some respite to a worn-out body and mind. I looked around for any sign of Tyler. I felt safer on the street because it gave me a good line of sight all around. Looking down the street, I could barely see the only other house in the neighborhood, several blocks down.

With a new plan in mind, I began to walk towards that house. I kept the wooded lots fully in my view as I went. A fear of Tyler—or anyone—lurking in those lots did slow me. As I got closer and closer, I tried to make out if anyone was home. Memories of the house I was approaching began to surface. I remembered the day when Tyler and I moved in. This had been our house, and Saris our only neighbor.

CHAPTER 5

Neighbors All Along

My mind began to unveil the reality of my personal life, shattering the daydream I'd been locked in for months. When I called Tyler my ex-husband, technically it wasn't true. We filed for divorce a year ago, but it's not finalized yet. Yes, that meant Saris and I were currently engaged in an affair. It was our being neighbors that had allowed Saris and I to meet in the first place. We had to keep our romance a secret because he's a well-respected preacher of a large church. I didn't want his parishioners to lose faith in him. So that late morning, I'd left a house that wasn't mine but felt like home while approaching a house that was actually mine but made me feel like a stranger every time I entered its doors.

The irony of that washed over me every time I would walk back home after a night of unbridled passion with Saris. Tyler had only found out about Saris a few weeks before David arrived to kill me. I'd blatantly told him during an argument. I was worried that Tyler would cause a fuss or strike me at that moment, but to my surprise, he didn't. In fact, in our last couple of months together, he didn't hit me anymore. Maybe he sensed a new strength growing in me. What's strange, in the past couple of months Tyler had actually showed hints of compassion towards me. That, however, was before I told him about Saris. Afterward, he kept a cold, almost respectful distance. The space he gave me was out of character for him. I guessed it could have been him just plotting to have me killed.

A most likely scenario: David had approached him sooner than I imagined. I didn't have a chance to ask David when he'd contacted Tyler—before I killed him with Atlas. Maybe Tyler had been on the fence about having me killed, until I told him about my relationship with Saris. Perhaps that gave him the extra motivation to have me killed.

Plagued by these questions, I arrived at the house. My keys were in my hand; I must have absentmindedly grabbed them when I left Saris's house. I opened the garage door. Tyler was not home, or at least his patrol car was not here. I still feared that he was hiding, watching somewhere. My goal was to get one of his guns and head to Saris's church on foot. His church lies about a mile down the road at the front of this neighborhood. If I was to get a weapon—Saris didn't own a gun—I had no choice but to stop here.

I was cautiously entering the house through the garage when I heard a car coming up the road. *Is Tyler coming home?* I wondered. My heart raced; my new fear was well warranted. Chances were high that it was Tyler. I knew I couldn't make it inside in time to get his gun because it required opening a combination lock. The combination was stored somewhere in Tyler's desk. Instead, I seized a baseball bat. A car turned into the driveway. A patrol car. *Dammit. It's Tyler.*

Confident I had already been spotted, I suddenly felt the need to charge at Tyler and somehow keep him from leaving his car. I ran toward the car, striking it forcefully with the bat.

The vehicle stopped, and Tyler screamed out, "Misty, what the fuck are you doing?"

I continued with the bat, making dents all over the car. The shatter-resistant windshield withstood the first strike of the bat. Tyler charged out of the patrol car, and I swung at him. Before I could connect, he firmly grabbed my incoming bat and pushed it forcefully back against me. I tumbled backward onto the ground, which kicked a plume of dust into my eyes. By the time I got to my knees, he had my hands cuffed in the front. Blinking out the dust and wiping my watering eyes, I was able to get a good look at him.

"Misty, what the fuck?" he demanded.

Dismayed, I tried and failed to pull my hands through the cuffs. I glared at Tyler.

Looking back he must have seen the rage on my face. His anger dissipated into a look of concern. "What happened to your neck and wrist?" he asked, seemingly unaware of what had happened to me.

I hadn't realized my neck was visibly bruised, but that was the last thing on my mind. I purposely didn't answer his question. I looked at him liked he should know. We both stood there, completely alone in the still-empty neighborhood. If I were to scream, it would go unnoticed. The only two houses were Saris's and ours. The church was too far up the street for anyone to hear a cry for help. The development's other streets, all carless, were separated from us by thick woods. My only hope, I realized, was that Saris would come home for lunch. Or maybe a realtor would drive by to put out a sign or show a lot. But that was a long shot. No realtor was likely to save me. Tyler could shoot me right here, and only nature would take notice. I stared at the gun in his holster, and decided I had nothing to lose from speaking the truth.

"I was afraid. That's why I hired David," I admitted, speaking between soft sobs.

Tyler stood there with a puzzled look. He lowered his eyebrows and asked, "David?" He genuinely looked like he didn't know who I was talking about.

"Or whatever name he used for you," I replied, taking another step backward.

Tyler noticed my fear. "Hold on," he said. "I'm not going to hurt you."

I stopped and let him proceed.

"Is that who hurt you?" he asked. "David?"

For a moment, we stood there in silence. I noticed stubble on Tyler's face, something I'd never seen on him before. I read sad concern in his brown eyes; he looked at me as if he was waiting for an answer. I waited, fully expecting an evil smirk to arise. I felt he was toying with me in some way.

I screamed, "You fucking know that! What kind of game are you playing here?" Before he could answer, I broke into a run. I darted across the street with handcuffs on, waiting for bullets to sear through my body. I entered the woods, hoping the trees would provide cover for any incoming rounds. The deeper I got, the safer I felt from being shot.

I could hear Tyler coming after me, yelling, "Misty? What are you doing?"

Despite being slightly overweight, I was a swift runner, but that didn't help. I could hear Tyler's footsteps catching up to me. The handcuffs slowed me down considerably, not to mention that Tyler was an avid runner.

My only hope was to hide. I spotted a thickly wooded area with lots of undergrowth. Maybe I could hide in there, I thought. Then I realized that going through the undergrowth I would loudly crackle over dead limbs, quickly revealing my location. Also, the tangled undergrowth would slow me down if I tried to get out. As I was trying to think this through, I could feel him close enough behind that I knew I couldn't hide.

I began to zig-zag, using the trees as a buffer behind me.

Tyler was just inches behind me, calling, "Misty, Misty, Misty," trying to sound calm and disarming.

My breathing was becoming labored. I felt I was hitting a runner's wall. *I have to keep going*, I told myself. Then I became dizzy, filled with dread. *Oh, no. I'm about to pass out.* I tripped. And then darkness.

CHAPTER 6

The Woods

I awoke feeling light, quick slaps on my face and hearing Tyler repeating, "Misty, wake up. Misty, wake up."

Why am I not dead? I wondered. This was his chance. My vision returned and I saw Tyler hovering over me.

Seeing that I was awake, he asked me, his tone soft and caring, "Are you OK?"

My mouth dry, I managed to utter, "Why didn't you kill me?"

His answer had a note of anger. "I'm not here to kill you. Why do you think that?" He moved back.

I sat up and listened.

"Can't you see I've changed?" he said. "Yes, I was a violent man in the past, maybe still a little, but I'm trying here." Tyler paused, with a long sigh. "I didn't know I scared you so much that you would think I would kill you." I caught a hint of despair in his voice, and of sympathy in his eyes.

I was taken aback by this display. *Is he being genuine?* I wondered.

"Give me your hands," he said, pulling a key out of his pocket. He leaned over to unlock my handcuffs. "You're free. You can go be with Saris. I understand why you can't be with me anymore. But before I let you go, I need to know: Is someone after you?" Tyler ran his finger gently over my bruised wrist. I saw deep concern on his face.

For a moment, this made me feel relaxed and safe. But the handcuffs were still on. Caution quickly welled back up. "Uncuff me, and I'll explain."

"OK," Tyler said. He unlocked my cuffs.

My hands free, I scrambled up to my feet and took several steps back. "I killed the man that was after me," I told him. If Tyler had hired David, and was still playing me, this would be the time for him to strike. I waited for him to jump up and chase me. Instead, he slowly stood up and took a step back, as if meaning to ease my fear.

"Again, who is David? Is that who hurt you?" Tyler was doing his best to sound deeply interested.

Tired of his games, I answered, "David's" the man you hired to kill me! And the man I hired last year to kill you! But I backed out minutes before he was scheduled to end you. That was a mistake!"

That did it. Tyler's pose shifted back to anger. *Here he goes*, I thought. His act, pretending to care, was about to dissipate. I had seen that pose too many times—before he struck me. "You tried to have me killed?" he shouted, shaking his head in disbelief. His head's motion slowed to a sweeping sadness. His stance became less aggressive; tears begin to well up in his eyes. He looked into my eyes and said, "You know what? I don't blame you for wanting me dead. Misty, I want to sincerely apologize for blaming you for Lily's death." He paused, almost in tears. "And I want to apologize for all the times I hurt you."

I stood there speechless, taken aback by what he was saying. *Is this remorse for hiring David to kill me?*

As if answering my thought, Tyler said, "But I never hired anyone to kill you. That means someone else hired this David," he said. "That someone else is out there."

Frustrated, I couldn't tell if Tyler was telling the truth. *Why would David lie to me? He was about to kill me!* Regardless, I started to feel a hint of sympathy towards Tyler.

"I still love you, despite everything," he tried to reassure me. That was something I hadn't heard since our daughter was killed.

I wanted to embrace him so badly, but I wasn't sure why. A minute ago, I had wished him dead. Now, If I had a loaded gun pointed at him, I couldn't pull the trigger. My murdering-Tyler spell had lifted—my hatred, gone. I pondered this. *Do I still love Tyler?* Maybe it was just a longing to feel safe, given the day I'd had.

Pure safety was something he'd given me, more than any man in my life had until he became the one I needed saving from. And when I say safety, I don't just mean physical protection from someone intent on doing me harm. I mean, safe from being alone. Today, I think I'm seeing the man that once gave me that safety. His hatred seemed to be gone and, with it, his accusatorial glare. Here was the man that wouldn't blame me, the man that wouldn't hit me, and the man that was part of my together. Here was the man I loved, I think.

Confused by my feelings, I kept my feet planted on the thick pine needles covering the ground. Trying to make sense of everything, I was distracted by a movement behind Tyler. Something was stirring in the woods.

Then I saw it, charging toward us. Ralph. I'd seen him in these woods before, during my nature walks. The last time, I had been far enough away to avoid any danger. Even so, fear of this creature had kept me from entering these woods alone afterward. When I told the story, I gave that nickname to the black bear I'd encountered: *Ralph.*

"Tyler, move!" I screamed.

His cop's instincts kicked in. He pivoted, pulled his gun out of his holster, and fired three times. It looked like all three shots hit the bear.

Ralph jerked slightly with each shot but didn't stop.

Tyler took a few steps back, pulling the trigger without any result. His gun was empty.

The bear shifted its focus towards me.

Why? Maybe I'd given "Ralph" the wrong name. It might be a mother bear, protecting her cub. I turned to run.

Once again, I began to zig-zag through the forest, hoping the trees would provide a buffer behind me. And once again, adrenaline flooded my body, causing a breathless heat that enveloped my face and ears. The bear's grunts and snorts seemed to be right in my ear. I knew I couldn't outrun it, so I purposely threw myself onto the ground, lying face down, hands wrapped over my head. I lifted my shoulders as high as I could to cover my exposed neck. Terrified, barely able to breathe, I felt death was certain.

I screamed, my face jammed into the soil as a claw sliced into my right leg and yanked me a few feet across the ground. Trying to protect my vital organs from more mauling, I flinched into a tight fetal position. Hot blood streamed from my wounded leg. I felt a sharp pain—like a thousand paper cuts—along with a desperate urge to tightly hold my position.

Curled up still, I could hear Tyler yell something, but my heart was pounding in my ear too loudly to make out his words. I tensed in anticipation of another blow, but agonizingly, uneventful seconds passed. Aware of my rapid blood loss, I was overpowered with an instinct to tend to my open wound, so I sat up, dangerously exposing myself. I took a deep breath, grabbed my blood-soaked jeans and tightly squeezed the cuts. I cried, one long wail, as if I could release the agony that gripped me like a tentacle.

It worked. Or at least I thought so. Survival instinct—or something—kicked in; the pain eased off slightly but still hummed, a high, piercing chord. My hands were disappearing under a fountain of red. I wasn't providing enough pressure, so I took off my shirt and wrapped it around my leg as a crude tourniquet. Sparks of torment flew every time I pressed the cloth against my scissored skin. Now wearing only a bra on top, I worked carefully at tightening the shirt, keeping it firmly in place over the wound.

Once I felt I had the bleeding under control, I looked around. *Where's Tyler? Where's the bear?* Nothing. I needed to find a better vantage point, I thought. Slowly and painstakingly, I lifted my body off the ground, favoring my injured leg, and quickly scanned my surroundings. Still nothing. Perplexed, I silently mouthed, *What the fuck?* Around me, the woods stood silent. I looked around for any sign of a struggle, any disturbed foliage, or any tracks of where they might have gone. The forest revealed no clues, no hint of a path.

So I hollered, "Tylerrr!... Tylerrr!... Tylerrr?" I stopped, waited for him to respond. Instead, the forest rustled faintly from a crisp, spring wind. Through my pain I felt both sorrow and worry for Tyler. This confused me. Only minutes before, I had genuinely believed he wanted me dead. Taking in everything that had happened, I surmised that Tyler had been telling the truth. That meant he didn't hire David to kill me. *Then who did?* My mind raced, considering possible suspects.

Could it have been a family member of Michael, the man who killed Lily? *If they didn't realize he deserved the death penalty,* it occurred to me, *they might think he's innocent. Could it have been someone in my family?* Sure, my sister and I don't get along, but I didn't think she would have me killed. *Would she?* I didn't have any other enemies that I could recall. Then my heart sunk with a sobering thought. *Was it Saris?*

My clawed leg demanded my attention again. The pain began to throb, forcing me to limp to a safer place. Luckily, I knew these woods from my nature walks. I quickly found the path leading back to Saris's house. I choose to go there because it was closer, and I needed to get my phone. I understood now that I had to involve the authorities after all, because I was still in danger. I had to plan what to tell the police. Obviously, I would leave out the fact that I had once hired David to kill Tyler. *I'm going to pretend like I didn't know the intruder,* I vowed. *And that he's still alive and on the loose.* In a way, he was still alive, because whoever it was who wanted me dead was still out there.

David's body also needed to be disposed of before I made the call to the police because I had moved it and attempted to burn him.

That would undoubtedly raise suspicions and the obvious question; *If he was already dead, why move him, and why burn him?* I did, however, felt confident if Tyler had survived the bear attack, he wouldn't tell the police about my association with David.

I limped along in painful steps, occasionally yelling, "Tylerrr." Nothing.

I approached the line where the forest gave way to Saris's large backyard and got a good look at the bay window where I'd been sitting that morning. Before emerging from the tree cover, I stopped to monitor Saris's house for any clues that he might have come home. Without warning, a panicky dread overtook me. I detected a familiar yet daunting smell. *David's cologne!* Terrified, I spun around, but saw nothing. Nobody. I exhaled in relief. Logic reminded me that David now lay in the downstairs shower.

Calming down, I thought through how I could smell a dead man's cologne; David must have watched me from this spot, and his smell still lingered. He must have spied on me reading in that window this morning before attempting to break into the bathroom. In a retrospective instinct, I thought I should have felt his eyes on me. That sent a chill of vulnerability through me. I hadn't been able to detect the stare of a dangerous man when it mattered. It was an instinct I didn't possess. That led to another question: *Could someone be watching me now and I couldn't tell?*

I limped out of the forest's protective shade. The sun warmed my chest, making me aware that I was still shirtless. That left me feeling even more exposed and vulnerable. With each step, I winced from the pain shooting up from my leg. Halfway across the yard, I stopped, seeing the back door slightly ajar. I knew the reason; David had come into the house through the back door. This still made me pause, still suspicious. Taking a breath, I summoned the courage to keep walking until I got to the door. I hesitated, listening for any sign that someone was inside. *I don't have to go all the way in,* I rationalized. *My phone is right there in the kitchen.* I rushed in and snatched open a kitchen drawer. My phone wasn't there. *That's where I put it!* I desperately searched all the drawers, coming up empty. Then I felt a presence in the room. A cold chill hit my arm and exploded all over my body, giving me far more than a shiver. I was feeling the aggressive approach of someone menacing. A little puff of wind told me the kitchen door was closing behind me. I turned to escape, but there he stood, just a few feet away. Now I could see it in his eyes. Something I couldn't have recognized before. The real man who wanted me dead.

Saris didn't even have to speak.

Chapter 7

Sleeping with the Devil

Holding up my phone, Saris approached me, saying, "Not only did you destroy my house, but you didn't—"

Before he could finish, I ran off into the living room. Behind me, I could hear "Die" before I bolted out the front door, screaming as loud as I could. "Help! Help! Help!" With my injured leg, I had barely gotten across the front yard and into the street before he captured me, enclosing my body in an aggressive hug.

"Tyler!" I yelled, before Saris threw me to the pavement. I crawled away from him and froze, afraid to run any farther because of the harm I feared he would inflict. I looked up, blinded by the late-afternoon sun in my face.

Saris looked down at me with a mocking expression. Almost laughing, he said, "Tyler? Is that who's going to save you? He's home. You want me to go get him?" Saris wasn't done with the mockery. "According to you, Tyler did nothing but hurt you."

That gave me a glimmer of hope. From his words, I assumed Saris wasn't aware of my exchange with Tyler in the woods. My hands on the warm pavement, I began to inch back again, slowly, so I didn't spark any alarm.

I tried to distract him with a question. "Why did you hire someone to kill me?" I wanted an answer to that lingering question because I felt like my safety net had been ripped from under me. I felt betrayed and duped. *Is his reputation that important?* I wondered.

Saris ignored my question. He leaned down and snatched me up by my bruised wrist and snarled, "Come on."

"Tyyyllllerrr! Help!" My voice echoed down the street. I hoped it would reach my house, where I hoped Tyler was still alive.

Saris dragged me across the yard.

I continued to scream. "Hellllp!"

He opened the front door and threw me into his house. I stumbled over the bloody statue that still lay on the floor. I almost tripped, which gave my feet momentum, propelling me to the bottom of the stairs and away from Saris. *Atlas saving me again?* The bloodied post with which I had stabbed David lay within reach. I seized it and flew up the stairs as fast as my wounded leg would allow. Saris's height and athletic prowess let him easily gain on me. I contemplated stopping abruptly, holding out the jagged post to stab him, but I knew Saris could overpower me just as David had. Instead, I took refuge in the bathroom.

I snatched the key out of the cracked bathroom door, feeling Saris's fingers grazing my shoulder an instant before I slammed the door behind me and locked it. This time I had the key, though I knew it had bought me only seconds. Saris could barge through the cracked door in no time. The crack *that David and I had caused just a fe* *hours before* striped the solid wooden door's center like a map of a river and its tributaries. The crack didn't go through to the other side. The wood was thick, but the barrier's integrity didn't matter against a man with murder on his to-do list.

I looked out the window and considered jumping but weighed the impact it would have on my legs. The jump could fracture my ankle, and probably reopen the wound from the bear's claw. The bathroom door started to shake. I turned to face the door and decided to stand my ground with the wooden post in hand. I stepped a little forward, crunching the shattered glass that lay strewn across the floor. I was ready to charge him.

The door stopped its shaking. A loud banging followed. The cracked river busted open and Saris's fist appeared. I took advantage of the opportunity in front of me. I grabbed his arm as he wiggled it, searching for the lock. He tried to pull back. I stabbed him in the wrist; the jagged wood went in deep, causing copious amounts of blood to pour out. Saris snatched his arm out before I could do any more damage. I peered carefully through the fist-shaped hole in the door. His blood dripped from the opening's top edge; his eyes glared at me.

Knowing how enraged he must be, I could tell Saris didn't want to leave my line of sight, but he must have desperately needed to tend to his wound. Improvising, just like I had out in the woods, he ripped off his shirt and wrapped it around his bloodied wrist.

What a difference a few hours make. Now, his body looked more savage than attractive. Underneath his usual suit was a beast that lived. I could see it now. Thousands of years of evolution and decorum had passed him by. He just knew how to play dress-up and to communicate. Seeing him shirtless reminded me I was, too. I had a clawed leg that I'd attended using the same method. A wound I wouldn't have gotten if Saris hadn't put me in that situation. I felt somewhat avenged, but still needed him to give me a reason for it all. So I asked him. "Why would you tell David to lie about who hired him to kill me?"

Then, before he could say anything, the answer hit me. He'd known there was a chance I might survive. If I did survive, I would prosecute Tyler, not him. Saris knew I was a fighter, despite the beatings I'd taken from Tyler. I could tell from Saris's face that he knew I had just come upon that answer. His eyes darted back at me, even more incensed that I was wise to him. I assumed he didn't want me to know that he thought I was a fighter.

That left me with an even more burning question. I asked again. "Why would you hire someone to kill me?" Before he could answer, I followed with, "Why didn't you just break it off? If you wanted to end it? I'm not so petty to where I would tell everyone about our affair."

Holding his arm with his bloodied shirt, he was about to answer, I could tell. I had a feeling the answer would incriminate him for something else. This was about more than his reputation. It was something more sinister.

Saris began to speak. "You were getting close to finding out, Misty." Realizing how vague that statement had been, he elaborated. "You were close to finding out that I killed your daughter."

That hit me like a fist to the gut, almost knocking the wind out of me.

My breathing elevated, moving my body with every breath, as I processed the thought: *I've been sleeping with the devil.* How could I not see who he was? The evil. The beast. The savagery. Until now, he had never showed me who he was. No suspicious statement ever came out of his mouth. *Not even a hair out of place in his behavior.*

Now my guard was up, behind reinforced walls of steel. Yet it was too late. The fortress of my heart had been breached, Trojan-horsed by a man I had loved—who had murdered my sweet, innocent little girl. *How? How did I let this happen?* Then I realized a truly cold person could play pretend and toy with someone's emotions until he got what he wanted. My fear had changed to fury. I wanted to charge through the door and push Saris down the stairs behind him, but I refrained. I let my unstoppable rage just brew, because I had another question.

"We didn't even live here when Lily was murdered." I focused my fury into the hand clenching the jagged wooden post. "It couldn't have been a coincidence that we ended up neighbors."

Calmly, he answered, "I'm surprised Tyler didn't uncover the fact that I own the entire neighborhood, or at least my father did. Hell, I have a church at the front of the subdivision. It was easy to casually push a realtor in your direction when I found out you were looking for a fresh start. I dropped the price of the house enough that Tyler couldn't refuse. My father's name was on the deed, Timothy Smith. He hadn't handed the development to me yet." He paused a moment as I took that in.

He went on, "That's right; my name is Smith, not Carlyle. I bet you're asking: Why do all this? Why would I kill your only daughter? Well, you have your husband, Tyler, to thank for all this. You didn't know my real name; and you didn't know that I was married."

This was all making me dizzy, but I kept my grip on the broken post, and kept my attention on this flood of horrifying information.

"My wife, Amelia, died four years ago," Saris said. "Under Tyler's custody. Yes, she had an opioid addiction. That led her to heroin. Tyler arrested her. Charged her with buying illicit substances, which I have no doubt she was."

Listening to this, of course, I knew Tyler's stance on drugs. I had always disagreed with him. Tyler had a tendency to blame the victim. I knew addicts were powerless in most cases. I believed that after a certain point addiction was a hijacking of the mind. But Tyler believed addicts just didn't have enough willpower and discipline. So he excoriated the victims. Still, even knowing this about Tyler, I couldn't accept Saris's logic. Nothing Tyler might have done could ever justify the killing of our innocent daughter.

"When your husband was putting my wife in handcuffs," Saris said, "he broke her arm. Then he threw her into the back of his patrol car. Frail as she was, he had no excuse for treating her that way. Maybe it had something to do with her being African-American. Amelia screamed from the pain, but he ignored her. And he didn't even take her to jail right away. He stopped to get himself some fast food."

That part didn't seem accurate to me. My husband was strict when it came to his diet. Saris also insinuated that Tyler had racist motives. That I couldn't be 100 percent sure of, but he hadn't shown any signs of racism during our marriage. Not that I ever saw, anyway. If he had, that would indeed have ended our marriage. Racism is an intolerable sin for me. So I was deeply skeptical as I listened to Saris trying to justify the unjustifiable.

"Amelia waited, in agony, in the back of the patrol car for the better part of an hour. When he finally got her to the station, he grabbed her by the arm, which he'd already broken. The pain was so bad she had a heart attack right there at the entrance to the police station. She asked for help, and he laughed at her. No one believed her until she was dead." I'd never heard Saris's voice sound so cold.

Numbly, I stared back at Saris through the fist-shaped hole in the door. I concluded his wife's death had made him the calculating psycho I saw in front of me.

What he said next proved I was right. "It wasn't long after Amelia died that I started stalking Tyler. And then his whole family. Your family. That's when I hired David to kill your daughter. Yep, I couldn't do it myself."

My stomach knotted up. David had been hired to kill Lily. Just like I had hired him to kill Tyler. And then he'd been hired to kill me. Evil seemed to circle my life, like a vulture picking at the carcass of my existence. Vomit was making its way up my throat when I reminded myself that David was dead. By now I was only half-listening to Saris.

"I was aware of your every move, Misty. I knew Tyler was blaming you for Lily's death. I introduced you to David without you even knowing. When he told me that you hired him to kill Tyler, I thought, Perfect! But then you backed out, Misty." He was pouting at me like a disgruntled child as he said this!

"That would have been perfect revenge for my wife."

Through the punched opening with jagged pieces of wood sticking out, I barely saw Saris squeezing the shirt wrapped around his wrist, responding to the pain. He grunted while saying, "Then I met you in person, and we bonded. It wasn't all fake, Misty. I did share your hatred towards Tyler. But after you lost your nerve about killing him, I noticed you were actually drifting back to him."

I stopped him. If David had abducted and killed Lily, what about the man on death row for that crime? "What about Michael?"

Saris gave a bitter laugh. "I, of course, set him up. Don't worry about him, Misty. He was a lowlife."

Done with his rationalizations, I snarled back, "My daughter was innocent in all of this! You're nothing but a coward who is going straight to hell! There is no justification here!"

Through the splintered hole, I watched Saris's muscles tense up. I could tell he was done communicating. So was I. He turned away and went down the stairs.

Was I free?

CHAPTER 8
Was I Free?

I didn't yet feel free.

My anger vanished into the cold dark reality. At this moment, in his house, it was Saris versus me. He wanted me dead. A human was hunting me on his own turf. All I had was this jagged post in my hand. Did I want him dead? I wasn't sure about that because I did want him to suffer. He couldn't suffer if he died. Also, he couldn't suffer the way I wanted him to if he killed me. So I had to summon strength.

I peered out the hole in the door, still locked. Still anxious, I expected Saris to run back up the stairs with a weapon of some sort. Something that could pry or smash this door open without his arm getting stabbed again. I needed to take advantage of his absence. I searched for ideas but came up with nothing. My only useful thought was that I couldn't be in this room when he broke in. I would be cornered and killed. I studied the locked doorknob with the wayward thought: *I don't yet feel free.*

With immense trepidation, I reached out and turned the key. I swung open the door, which creaked, the only noise in the house. Saris had to hear it. I held my jagged post in defense and stepped out of the bathroom's relative safety

I scanned the open hallway and down the stairs. With each step, I consoled my worried mind: *I have plenty of time to run back into the bathroom if Saris comes charging up.* Through an open bedroom door, I saw the unmade bed where we'd had sex that morning. I couldn't believe that was just a few hours ago. This day already felt like a lifetime of turmoil rolled into one. Each step away from the bathroom heightened my anxiety, but I knew staying in there wouldn't save me, just buy me time.

With the bloodied post firmly in hand, I turned to go down the stairs. I pressed my side against the wall while I cautiously took each step down. This stance offered me a partial view into the living room, kitchen, and dining room, but with a blind spot along the side of the stairs. I tried to peer over the railing, but I wasn't tall enough, and was too far back. Saris could be squatting there, and I couldn't see. Out of caution, I kept my feet close to the wall.

The hushed house offered no clues to where he might be hiding. I paused halfway down to let my breathing slow. For most of the day, I had felt fear, but this felt different. This time, it wasn't just about me. If I wasn't smart in my actions, I couldn't avenge Lily's death. It was more than my own survival at play now. I had the weight of my daughter's life on me, which since her birth, had always been there in some form. And more so now after her death. I wanted to punish Saris, but not in revenge. Revenge felt petty, like I was trying to even a score in a game. I desperately wanted justice, in whatever form that took.

Suddenly, I was weeping. I'd been sleeping with my daughter's killer. Her legacy of life had survived within me, and yet I had ended up in the arms of her monster. I continued down the rabbit hole of self-torture. *How could I not know he was so diabolical? Was it pure lust—nothing but sex—that drove me to him?* I hoped with all hopes it had been more than that. I like to think I had more self-control. Or had my mind been hijacked, like an addict? Regardless, I felt weak because I'd caved to Saris. I was left with: *Why did I do it—for sex or companionship?* The answer would elude me as I chased after it night after sleepless night, cross-examining every step I'd taken to Saris's bed. If I even survived, of course.

The tears almost blinded me, putting me in mortal peril.

To survive for Lily, I knew I needed to control my emotions. So I subdued my crying to regain focus on my hearing and sight. I listened and looked intently around the house. The setting sun was deeply angled down, shining through the windows and illuminating the floors in pockets. Particles of dust drifted in the fleeting light. Throughout the house, darkness was slowly creeping out of the corners. That made me realize no lights were turned on. Hopelessly, I looked at the front door. Trying to run out of it was a bad idea, especially given my injured leg. Halfway down the stairs, back against the wall, I inhaled quietly.

At my feet, the silence shattered. I withdrew in shock as Saris leaped out of the blind spot beside the stairs. He threw himself through the gap in the broken railing. Before I could think about running, his hands possessed my legs like a demon, violently snatching me off my feet. I crashed backward hitting my back against the stairs. I dropped the bloodied post.

He tugged and pulled me down as I kicked for my life, but his firm grip limited the scope and impact of my kicks. The splintered remnants of the railing cut through my pants and into my soft flesh. The sharp wood penetrated the back of my thigh. I couldn't help but wail in anguish as the pain of being dragged over the broken wood was added to the agony of my bear-clawed leg.

About to topple off the stairs, eyes watering from the hurt, I barely noticed the bloody shirt wrapped around the hand Saris had clamped around my ankle. A way to fight back presented itself. I violently twisted my foot, hoping that would cause him enough pain that he'd let go. Below me sounded a loud cracking of wood, and Saris dipped away, unclenching my ankle. Peering over, I saw books tumbling around him. His feet had been on the bookshelf inset under the stairway, which had given him the reach he needed to grab my legs. But in the struggle, the wooden shelves had given way under his weight. He lay below me, unconscious, a mountain of books around and on top of him.

I looked again towards the front door, the door to freedom, with the lingering question: could I run away fast enough before Saris wakes? In the corner of my eye, I could see Saris flickering back to life, fighting the temporary paralysis from his fall. *There goes my chance.* He was too close to the foot of the stairs. I wouldn't make it.

Saris's awakening sent trains of terror racing through my veins. My heart unleashed its machinery, my motor systems called to action. Act I did. I lifted my thigh off the splintered post, leaving a puddle of blood behind. I gritted my teeth and sucked in my breath to help me cope with the pain. I needed to move.

Back on my feet, I hobbled up, in agony with each step. My outward movements couldn't match the speed I felt roaring inside me. Determination and adrenaline made me want to move faster, but my shredded legs wouldn't allow it. Saris's shoes clicked on the floor amid the thumping of books falling off his body. The killer was upright again, ready to charge. And charge he did. The sound of him accelerated the trains running through my system, now bullet trains, urging me to speed as my shredded legs moved at a snail's pace.

I was living the nightmare of moving in slow motion from someone chasing me. *Am I dreaming?* Oh, how I wished I was dreaming. The torment that screamed from my body awakened me to the reality that I wasn't. At the top of the stairs I spotted the porcelain toilet tank lid I had dropped during my earlier battle with David.

Saris was on the bottom step.

Taking my last step to the top, I exhaled from the pain, lifted the heavy lid with both hands and turned to face him. A deja vu moment swept over me; just hours ago, David had been in a similar position. I threw the lid towards Saris, but he dodged the impact. The porcelain shattered, fragments flying through the stair rail. I promptly turned and fled into the bathroom again.

For the third time today, I locked myself in this bathroom. The key still inside the lock. Watching the hole in the door, waiting for Saris's hand to come through again, I realized I didn't have my post this time. My back thigh seized up with the fresh pain from the splintered wood Saris had just dragged me across. The blood was saturating my jeans. Time for another tourniquet; I took hold of a towel and tied it around my thigh, hoping it would stop this new bleeding. It helped, but didn't entirely check it. I shifted to other priorities: *How can I fight Saris?*

I searched the room desperately for a weapon with an eye still on that hole. Shattered glass lay everywhere. In the glittering ruins, I glimpsed a potential weapon. I looked again, and a long shard stood out amongst the rest. *A knife.* I started to clench the glass but realized the danger. Seizing a hand towel, I wrapped it around the bottom of the makeshift knife. It still felt sharp against my hand but protected me enough to do the job. My new weapon ready, I hunched my body and faced the door.

Saris's footsteps approached the door. Sweat dripped from my face. He stopped just outside the door, and only the sound of my heart pounding in my ear remained. I still felt the trains chugging along, but less alarmingly. A full minute passed and I didn't blink. My eyes were frozen upon the hole in the door. No sound. Nothing. Not even breathing. The anticipation of a loud burst had me on edge. My hand shook, almost dropping my makeshift knife.

I stepped back for a moment before psyching myself out. I kept a watchful eye on the opening. But darkness was enveloping the room, which made it difficult to see. I flipped the light switch with no result; I kept trying, still no effect. He must have turned off the power, I reasoned, to give himself the upper hand. With the impending darkness, I grew more and more impatient. Realizing how close the doorknob was to the hole, I took a closer position to prevent his hand from sneaking through and unlocking it.

I trembled, fearful about the oncoming fight for my life. I wasn't confident I could win. Saris was tall and strong. Then the door awoke with a fresh crackling noise and a new crack emerged, closer to the knob. Peering through the hole, I saw a hammer in his hand, prying at the door.

My chest heaved; my breathing sped up. Every molecule of me down to droplets of sweat told me to get out and away from him. I could feel the seconds rocketing toward my death. I turned to face the room's only window. *My only way out.* The first two times I was in here, I decided against jumping due to its height. This time, I felt I had no other choice.

I scoured the bathroom for something to help me jump and minimize the impact on my feet. My search ended in frustration that there wasn't anything to tie together, like a rope, to lower me. Meanwhile, Saris was tearing further into the door, giving me little time to plan. Overpowered by urgency, I dropped my makeshift knife and stepped onto the toilet seat, which gave me a step onto a drawer in the vanity beside it. I stood on the drawer and pulled myself up onto the windowsill. I swung both my legs over and took a good look down. I swallowed hard, dreading a long fall that could very well break my legs or kill me. Then I noticed a protruding nail in the window frame. An idea formed.

I unhooked my bra and pierced one end with the nail; I folded the end over and stabbed it again. I decided to leap using the bra as a rope. I didn't expect it to hold me long but hopefully long enough to slow my fall. Sucking in my breath and looking down at the manicured grass, I realized a towel would have worked better, but it was too late now. No time to go back into the bathroom or even unwrap the towel around my leg; because at that moment the door busted open and Saris came charging. Gripping the bottom of my bra, I edged myself off the windowsill and jumped.

The garment stopped me for one second before ripping and giving way. I landed hard on my feet; a stinging pain shot up my legs, which buckled. I collapsed to the ground. For a few seconds, I couldn't get up but desperately wanted to. An inch from my face, a hammer struck the ground.

Saris had missed. I let out a thankful sigh. I heard him bark some kind of threat from the window before dipping back into the house. I had to get moving before he got downstairs. Shaking from the impact on my legs, and weak from all the injuries I'd suffered, I staggered to my feet and ran. Wobbly at first, eventually I broke into a sprint across the yard and disappeared into the dark woods. Night had arrived. Again, I was hit with the thought, *Am I free?*

I wanted it to no longer be a question.

CHAPTER 9
Final Resting Place

My exposed breasts bounced uncomfortably as I trotted through the darkened forest. Even though it might have saved me, I wished I still had that D-cup bra. My eyes had adjusted enough to let me avoid trees or fallen logs in front of me. The clear moonlight helped, glimmering through the canopy in spots. I did have a sense of where these woods emptied onto the busy highway, but the darkness made it more difficult to find the familiar landmarks that would guide me.

After a few more minutes, I stopped to catch my breath and to listen. Only the sounds of insects emanated from the woods around me. Not hearing the crunch of Saris's footsteps, I felt somewhat safe. Over time, the trees had deposited enough leaves, pine straw and branches that it was nearly impossible to walk without making a sound, especially in the night.

Thinking back, I was surprised I could run after my jump from the window. Maybe the bra had helped, but being topless made me feel uneasy. I desperately wanted to cover myself, but the forest offered me nothing. I kept my arms folded over my chest as I crept forward.

Through the trees, I saw a small opening a few feet away. I stepped into the moonlit clearing, which allowed me to see better. My legs still throbbed. I checked my wounds; the shirt remained tied around my bear-clawed leg. Running my fingers along the shirt, feeling for fresh blood, I sighed in relief that the bleeding had stopped. Next I checked my thigh, unwrapping the towel from the cuts the splintered wood had inflicted. The towel wasn't doing much; the jeans were pressed into my skin, the dried blood acting as an adhesive. I felt across the crusty red patch and found this, too, had stopped bleeding. My lower back was aching from my falls on the stairs, but it was nothing I couldn't handle at the moment. A hope that I could survive began to rise—until I heard a sound.

It was a man's voice. "Misty …" My name floated, ghostly, through the air. I started to shiver from fright, not the chill night air. Readying myself for a battle, I grabbed a branch with a sharp end where it had broken. I stood still and listened. A leaf descended and landed on my bare breast. Frozen in my stance, I didn't brush it off. Peering into the dark shadows under the trees, I spotted something illuminated in a patch of moonlight. The whites of two eyes glared back at me.

"Ahhhhhhhh—" I screamed, involuntarily, unable to move. Frozen in fear, I gazed at this thing jumping through the shadows and approaching me. The moonlight confirmed that it was a man. His hands extended, covered my mouth, and silenced my scream. I was able finally to focus on his face.

It was Tyler. Dizzy from my scare, I went limp and fell into his arms. In Tyler's embrace, I felt safe. Less alone.

Tyler shifted me gently off him, holding me out at arm's length and took a good look at me. Noticing I was shirtless, he shrugged off his uniform jacket and offered it to me. I nodded, accepting the offer. Carefully, remembering my bruised wrist, he lifted my arm, helping me into his warm jacket and zipping it closed. I felt protected from the elements and the world. His macho presence standing before me, Tyler was like a knight eager to defend his lady. I could see the regret in his eyes for not having been there to save me from all that I'd endured today. He pushed my hair back from my face.

Softly, I asked him, "The bear? I thought you were dead."

In a whisper, he responded, "I managed to outrun it. After a few seconds, it collapsed. From my gunshots. But by then I didn't know where I was. I don't know these woods like you do, so I've been lost this whole time. I couldn't call for help because I left my phone and two-way in the patrol car when I ran after you." He paused with a question for which he seemed to know the answer. "Saris is after you, isn't he?"

With a resounding "Yes!" I answered, "Not only that, he hired David. To kill our Lily!"

I watched Tyler's reaction dance between confusion and anger before settling on fury. A break in the trees allowed the moonlight to spotlight his face. He wore not the face of an angry cop but the face of a furious father. Our eyes met in shared outrage at this knowledge. Our enemy's identity became clear. Saris would have to pay. Tyler's fury ebbed while he reached his hand out and touched my cheek.

Confidently, he said, "Misty, we're going to punish him and finally move on with our lives."

I agreed wholeheartedly in his statement. Anticipating his next question, I said, "He told me he killed Lily because he blames you for killing his wife, Amelia Smith, four years ago."

Tyler's expression acknowledged he knew who Amelia was. His manner softened. With regret in his voice, he said, "I did kill Amelia. I mean, not directly or intentionally. When I arrested her that night, she resisted—strongly. I had to force her into the car. And I didn't take her to the station right away because I was busy interrogating her about who'd sold her the heroin." He shook his head. "I wasn't satisfied just busting one junkie; I wanted to arrest her dealer, too. But after about an hour of questioning, I wasn't getting anywhere, so I gave up. Once we got to the station, she died right there in the parking lot. I'd put her under extra duress that night. I know that. It was because I had such high expectations—for everyone. So Saris may be right. I could have been the cause of Amelia's heart attack."

I could hear the lump in Tyler's throat as he admitted, "That incident became a turning point in my way of thinking. I realized drug addiction passes a point in people to where—no matter how strong someone's willpower is—they can't stop. Not unless they're forced by death or rehab. It took that night—and Lily dying—for me to really understand addiction because I wanted to escape reality by whatever means necessary."

Then he looked at me and admitted something else. "Despite what I'd figured out about addiction," he said, "I fell into it myself. After Lily, I started to drink. A lot. It's only been a couple of months ago that I stopped."

I had been completely unaware of this, even when we were still together. He'd hidden his drinking well. "Each day has been a struggle to stay sober. I'm in no way using this as an excuse, but when I started drinking, that's when I started to hit you." Tyler's remorseful eyes peered through the moonlight and into my soul. All anger, fear, and doubt that I held toward him evaporated; back were the schoolgirl feelings that fluttered inside. He was … is the love of my life, and in my recent despair, I had actually wanted him dead.

My next words were genuine. "I'm sorry I wanted you dead. I don't know what I was thinking—"

"No!" Tyler stopped me. "Don't you feel bad for wanting me dead. I didn't make you feel safe, and you were mourning our daughter's sudden death. It's ironic; I'm a police officer, and I didn't make you feel safe." He stepped closer and looked more intently into my eyes. "Once we get through this, I hope we can make amends, and I hope you can trust me again. I meant it earlier: I love you, Misty. I never stopped loving you, not even in our darkest days, and we had some dark days. If you don't want to be with me, that's fine. I can help you pursue whatever dream or goal you might have going forward. I'm here for you either way."

Tyler's words moved me to reach out. I kissed him, maybe for the last time. I wasn't sure how this night would play out.

He kissed me back more passionately, like he'd been eager to do this for months.

I could hear the feminists in my head say, *He hit and controlled you for over two years, and now you're taking him back.* Yet mentally I defended myself. Nobody else could understand the context; everything in this world is not always black and white.

Fully engaged in a deep sensual kiss, a rising urge helped me forget the pain in my legs. Given my precarious situation, I was shocked by my arousal. I was sure Saris was out there in the forest still searching for me. *We need to flee.* But my lips couldn't depart. *We need to find the road. No, wait, I need this now. Him now.* I didn't know how deprived I was of Tyler's affections until this moment when my logical thought surrendered to him. I couldn't unlock from him. I couldn't flee—even though I knew danger lurked.

Caught up in the kissing, I think we both realized this might be our last time. Knowing how fleeting it all was kept us going. Even our vanity didn't even matter; I had never looked as bad as I did then. On a normal day, low self-esteem would have suppressed any desire to have sex. Maybe it is an instinct built into us by nature. If a couple were about to embark on a dangerous mission, pheromones would increase.

Whatever the reason, I was horny, and so was Tyler. I felt him against me. His lips moved across my cheek, and found my neck. I leaned my head in and pushed my body more tightly against his. Digging my hands into the jacket's pockets, I opened it, exposing my breasts, the nipples hard.

Tyler rolled his crisp white T-shirt over his head and threw it onto a tree branch.

I rubbed my fingers against his newly exposed skin, taut over his well-muscled body. He emitted a sweet musk that provoked my desire. We hadn't had sex in three years. I'd forgotten how much I once enjoyed intercourse with him. The memories flooded back, arousing me more. His lips left my neck, as his hands cupped my breasts. Nuzzling his head against my chest, he kissed and flicked his tongue around a nipple. I started to moan, but with a hand, he suppressed my voice. He wanted me to remain quiet because we were still in danger. I didn't feel distracted. Instead, my senses felt heightened.

If Saris did stumble upon us in this position, I would enjoy parading it in his face. For the first time since this morning, I didn't feel scared. It was the two of us against one. Tyler removed his hand from my mouth, and I felt my pants coming undone. He carefully folded the top of my jeans down, stopping at my wounded thigh. When it came to my underwear, Tyler's hand turned savage, prying them until they suffered a rip, dropping on my folded-out jeans. At the sound of his pants unzipping, my exposed skin vibrated in anticipation. Slowly, he pressed himself into me. No longer accustomed to his girth, I was really feeling Tyler's pressure.

Once his motion started, I felt some discomfort, but Tyler was the first pain I had enjoyed today. With each thrust, I grew wetter and wetter. Then all the other physical and emotional hurt dwindled into a joyful race to climax. Our sex seemed barbaric, like we were caught in a different time. I also sensed that this was how sex was supposed to feel. The backdrop of the woods helped inform me about my ancestors. In the depths of nature, and not in the confines of steel and concrete, copulation happened frequently and over generations. I felt at one with nature, more so than I did during one of my walks. The forest seemed to blanket us momentarily from the turmoil of the day. It all felt so good, and Tyler felt so right. An upsurge of good feelings and revelations flooded through me.

On one of the hardest days of my life, I climaxed for the third time. This climax was sweeter, better, more explosive. His hand cupped over my mouth again, but the squeal of my voice made its way through. I tasted him. His salty sweaty hand. I loved the taste of him. I loved him. I shook. For long seconds I shook. I could barely stand. I wanted to lie with him on the forest floor. I didn't care what little creatures might scurry beneath us. All fear was gone, absent from my mind. The trains had stopped. Tyler squeezed me into his sculpted physique until I no longer shook. Then I remembered time. We didn't have much time. The reverie ended.

I pulled up my torn underwear, cutting my eyes at Tyler for ripping them at the seams.

He just smiled back in a half-cocked way.

Buttoning my pants helped hold in the stretched-out panties. I closed the police jacket over my chest again. Tyler and I looked at each other, astonished that we had just had sex. I don't know about him, but my mind felt clearer. I was ready to go into battle with Saris. Tyler seemed more relaxed and ready, as well.

But before we could devise a plan against Saris, a sound silenced us. A limb snapped, echoing through the woods.

Tyler did have a gun, but he had used his only three rounds on the bear.

Even so, I pointed to the pistol, still holstered at waist, indicating he could bluff with it.

He nodded in agreement. Pulling his gun, Tyler pointed it into the darkness.

Silently, we scanned the forest around us, waiting for the dark to move. I was stopped by the moon's ray that unveiled a face, poking out from the trees ahead. *Saris!* Like a predator, he stepped into the pale light.

Locking eyes with me, Saris pounced with a hammer in his hand.

I pointed toward him and screamed. "Saris!"

At first, Tyler stood still.

I sensed that he wanted to stay and fight. My confidence started to disappear and I grabbed Tyler's arm, tugging him into a run. I wasn't ready for us to engage in hand-to-hand combat with Saris. He had a hammer, and Tyler had me, but I didn't want to chance it.

Tyler and I carefully maneuvered through the night, avoiding branches and tripping hazards. I guided him because I knew where I was and how to get to the road. By now, though, the pain in my clawed leg had erupted again, stiffening my movements and slowing me to a limp.

Tyler tried to lift me into his arms, but I refused his help. Then, hearing Saris get closer, I forfeited my pride and let Tyler carry me. His lean torso and strong, massive upper body allowed us to gain ground against Saris. But I was only guessing, based on the fact I couldn't hear Saris running behind us anymore. Tyler's heaving breaths could be muffling his deadly approach. I was terrified that the hammer he held, at any moment, might clock us in the head. And into unconsciousness. And then death. So I looked behind us. There was no sign of Saris. Now I feared he had taken a different route and would pop out in front of us. Even in Tyler's bouncing arms, I refocused on our surroundings and pointed out the way to go as he ran.

"This way, babe. That way. Turn here. Right here."

Finally, our street came into view, and Tyler maneuvered us around the last trees. He crossed the ditch and onto the pavement and gently placed me on my feet. We looked around and saw that we were halfway between our house and Saris's. Yellow streetlights illuminated both front yards, the only two outside lights in the vast, empty neighborhood. Tyler pulled his keys out of his pockets, and we ran towards our house. I endured the pain from my leg and pretended I could run at full speed; this mindset helped some—I didn't limp— but I still lagged behind. Tyler gripped my arm to help me keep up, and I ran alongside him. I could see Tyler's patrol car still in the driveway. Safety was in sight.

But at any minute, I expected Saris to burst out of those woods and thwart our escape. Our pace quickened as we got closer to the car, our paths dividing as he went for the driver's seat and I pushed myself toward the passenger seat. We entered the car at the same time. He locked the doors. Remembering the horror movies I'd watched as a teenager, I checked the back seats. *All clear.* I sighed in relief.

Tyler cranked the car and picked up his portable police radio to call for help. Abruptly, the side window shattered into his lap. A blunt object hit him in the head, and he dropped the radio. I grabbed for it as a hammer pulled back from Tyler's bloodied face. I let out a scream of despair; Tyler sat unresponsive. Through the shattered glass, Saris appeared with a vicious grin. He leaned into the window to get a hold of me.

As he reached out, I pressed a button on the side of the radio and screamed into it, "Help, send help!" Unfamiliar with the device, I wasn't sure if my cry for help went through. Straining over Tyler to reach me, Saris pinched my jacket, and I yanked him off. I tried to carry the radio out of the car, but a tightly coiled cord kept it tied to the dashboard. Leaving Tyler and the radio, I bolted away, scurrying into the wooded lot beside our house. I stopped a few feet from the tree line and looked back. The yellow streetlight spilled light into the driveway, and I could see Saris still standing beside the patrol car. He was still bare-chested, his shirt wrapped around his wrist.

I wanted him to chase me and leave Tyler alone. I prayed that Tyler was just unconscious.

Saris smirked and began to saunter toward the tree line. "Misty, Misty, come out, come out wherever you are." He taunted me, like we were playing a childhood game of hide and go seek.

Hoping to lure him away from Tyler, I engaged him with, "I'm here," revealing my location.

Saris stormed toward the sound of my voice.

I turned to run, but my legs were entangled in fallen limbs. The rustling of branches and leaves signaled even more clearly where I was. Struggling to pull my feet free, I felt a vicious blow from the hammer. For a few seconds, I tried to stay awake, but dizzily wobbled and fell. To my death. *My final resting place.* All I saw was Lily's heavenly face.

CHAPTER 10

Tyler

Tyler awakened, his head fuzzy, with an intense pain from the hammer blow to his forehead. He felt his hands suspended overhead, encircled with metal. He realized he was handcuffed onto a bed. A crumpled comforter lifted his back at an uncomfortable angle. Darkness surrounded him as he scanned the room. Dimly visible, the familiar decor told him he was in his own bedroom.

He strained at his cuffed hands, which yielded no result. Looking to his left and right, Tyler saw both hands were locked to the bed's headboard. He surmised that Saris had found both pairs of handcuffs on his belt and used them on him.

The only light in the room was the bedside clock; 11:16 p.m., the yellow light told him. The clear, moonlit night helped brighten the window curtains to a dark blue against the room's blackness. As he lay, unable to move, Tyler worried about Misty's fate. A feeling pervaded him: *Misty is dead.*

The thought left him with a crushing weight of guilt. Tyler felt responsible for all the events that had led to today. He reflected on the night, four years ago, when Amelia Smith had died while in his custody. Just before that day's police shift began, he had surveyed one of his properties for a future housing development, thinking of all the hurdles he'd have to overcome to transform it from dense woods into homes. Something had agitated him as he watched the sunset on his property that evening. It was more than the challenge to develop this land, and more than the constant swatting away of mosquitos that left his arms swollen with bites.

He grew mad at the world and his thoughts turned to the street addicts he dealt with almost daily. It was more than a professional issue; it was personal. His parents had struggled with a stint of drug addiction during his childhood. Both had sobered up and recovered after getting in trouble with the law. Tyler had presumed all addicts needed swift and tough action to make them stop. The more he thought about it that night, the more his agitation grew. That was why Tyler had started his night shift boiling mad.

He had been on patrol less than an hour when he spotted Amelia under a dim streetlight. She was leaning against a sign that spelled "Greenland Court," the entrance to a small trailer park. It consisted of eleven rusted single-wides manufactured sometime in the 1970s or 1980s. The yards were overgrown and littered with broken swing sets and derelict cars stripped down to the frame. Most of the area's manufactured home communities housed decent, working-class families, but this one stood out as a cesspool of crime.

Tyler thought this was an excellent place to start his own personal war on drugs, and Amelia was the first enemy he saw. "Ma'am," he confronted her. "What are you doing?"

"I'm waiting on my husband," she declared, a phone clutched in one hand. He knew right away that she was high and had just injected herself. A length of rubber tubing was still wrapped around her arm, and a syringe protruded from her jeans pocket. No need for a body search; the paraphernalia were all there in plain view.

Stepping out of his patrol car, he declared, "Ma'am, you are under arrest."

"What for?"

"Look at your arm."

Behind her glazed eyes, he saw defeat. In this moment, Tyler's anger drained away. He felt for her, seeing her as a victim of the pharmaceutical industry's unchecked powers. From her clothing and demeanor, his cop's instinct told him, she came from a middle-class background, probably well educated, and definitely new to this life. Another lost soul, he thought. He wanted to help her, like his parents had been helped.

Between Amelia's fingers and her phone, Tyler saw a tiny zip-lock bag. And inside the plastic, a white powder. Heroin, no doubt.

Tyler took a step closer to Amelia and said, "Ma'am, I'm going to have to book you for possession." As he spoke, he effortlessly snapped handcuffs around her wrists.

Amelia flew into a rage, punching against the restraints. She cussed and thrashed about while Tyler wrestled her into his car. His final, brutal shove would later haunt him with a question: Was that push necessary? Even as he locked her into the back seat, he thought he could have gotten her in more gently, given that he was twice her size and four times her strength.

For at least five minutes after he took off from Greenland Court, she screamed obscenities at him. By now, Tyler had lost his rage, and she couldn't rile him up even after calling him every vile term in the book. Even so, he held onto his self-declared war on drugs. For an hour, he drove Amelia around town, interrogating her about where she had bought the heroin.

"Which trailer in Greenland Court, if it was Greenland Court? What did the man or woman look like? Was his name Brad? The guy who goes by 'Snake' because of his serpent tattoos?" His questions went on and on.

He badly wanted to catch the man nicknamed Snake, assuming he was Amelia's drug dealer. But he got nowhere. Giving up on his interrogation, Tyler turned his car into the police station's back lot. His war-on-drugs crusade was waning, his demeanor ebbing back into the gentle family man Tyler usually was.

Tyler unlocked the car's back door to guide Amelia out, but she began thrashing again, directing more coarse language at him. He summoned up all his training to keep himself under control as he tried to calm and steady her. Then, without warning, she fell silent and froze, collapsing before him. Tyler yelled for help. He scooped his arm under her body to lift her. She hung limp in his arms. Getting a good look at her face, he saw her eyes were rolled back. No breathing at all.

Two officers rushed out and took her from Tyler. One performed CPR until an ambulance arrived.

Guilt smacked Tyler. The timespan that followed would become a blackout to him. Afterward, he couldn't remember how his colleagues had questioned him about this arrest. He couldn't remember his drive home that night. What he did remember was opening the door to his house and greeting Misty.

He never understood why he'd gotten so irate about the drug issue that evening, and why it had come all at once. It was a question he had asked himself daily ever since.

From that day forward, he'd kept his emotions in check while on duty, even after Lily died. But in the days and months after Lily's death, he'd inflicted hell at home on Misty, either physically or emotionally. *No wonder she hired someone to kill me.* No matter how good a police officer he'd been, it wasn't enough to atone for his behavior.

Now he understood that his actions that night had set off a chain of events that ensued to this day. He felt not only Amelia's blood on his hands, but also his daughter's—and now his wife Misty's, too.

Tyler's mind snapped back into focus, as he detected a shadowy figure in the corner of the room.

The darkness moved to the bed's edge. A man spoke. "You watch, now. I'll be back to kill you." Tyler recognized Saris's voice. Then in front of the bed the TV came on, displaying a homemade video. In it were a newlywed couple. It was Amelia and Saris. A closeup showed them grinning at each other, with loving eyes. With a caress of his thumb, Saris gently wiped frosting from the wedding cake off Amelia's lips.

Tyler knew what Saris was doing. He yelled, "I'm truly sorry for how I handled your wife."

Turning back from the doorway, Saris responded, coldly, "I'm not sorry for killing yours." His shadow disappeared into the hallway.

Angered and helpless, Tyler tugged again at the cuffs. The headboard's mahogany posts, barely scratched, held him captive. Amelia's voice came through the TV, successfully stoking guilt. Knowing Misty was dead he let go of the tension in his body. It decompressed, limply, surrendering. At that moment, the will to live left him. Succumbing to Saris's mental torture, Tyler stared blankly at the television. He waited patiently for death.

Chapter 11

In Bed

"Mom." Her hand held out, Lily's angelic voice reverberated.

"I'm here. Mom's here," I said, running to embrace my daughter.

The Devil stepped in front of me, blocking my path to Lily. The horned demon taunted me as I tried to move around him. Suddenly, a black void engulfed my surroundings, extinguishing Lily's light. Hope gave way to despair. I could feel the Devil's lips against mine as a new, dimmer light appeared. His lips withdrew, and I heard a voice.

"Misty, I'm going to miss you when you're dead." Saris hovered inches from my face.

In a panic, I sat up.

He backed away, giving me room to process. I was in Saris's bed. I ripped the cotton sheet off my legs. I was wearing a bra again—different from the one I'd left dangling from the bathroom window.

My underwear had been changed as well, but I had no other clothing on. In just my underwear, half naked, I felt violated and exposed.

I did notice my wounds had been cleaned and bandaged, which left me wondering how long I had been unconscious and whether he had done anything else to me. I felt frozen in place. If I tried to get away, I knew he would overpower me.

The bedroom's overhead light shone brightly under the spinning ceiling fan. Sprawled on Saris's king-size bed, the centerpiece of his second-floor master bedroom, I coiled into a defensive position. My knees met my breasts while my toes gripped the recently laundered sheets. This bed, this room, which had been filled with warmth and happiness this morning, were now full of my deep hatred for the man who sat at my side.

Saris leaned back and grabbed a glass of water from the nightstand. "Here, drink this. You're dehydrated."

My parched lips couldn't say no. I was still stunned to be alive. I reached out and seized the drink. Chugging the water, I realized I was shaking. Once again, the trains were back, racing and rattling through me. Saris was still shirtless, but this time his wrist was properly bandaged. My eyes shifted to his legs, noting his pants were missing. Then I became aware of the erection protruding through his boxer briefs. I jolted back in alarm and threw the emptied plastic cup at him.

He snatched my arms and tried to sound reassuring as he spoke. "I'm not going to rape you. I just want to spend one more night with you, platonically. Before I kill you in the morning." He said that last part almost off-handedly, without emphasis. Mindful of my fear, I figured, he didn't want me to fight back. Saris's face inched closer to mine like he was going to kiss me.

"I was kissing you while you slept; that's why I'm hard," he said bluntly. His head cocked to the side, he gave me a pitiful glare. "Misty, you're innocent in all of this."

That was too much. I flew into a tirade. "So was Lily! It takes some kind of monster to kill a thirteen-year-old girl! The gates of hell will open to you, an eternity in hell, for revenge." Shaking my head at his stupidity, I went on, "You made a bad trade."

Saris unleashed my arms and slapped me across the face. My head bounced to the side before I turned it back up to meet his eyes. He remained inches away. With a menacing growl, he said, "You try anything, and I will kill you right now!" His blue eyes froze on me.

His icy threat punctured my rage, replacing it with sinking dread.

He leaned back away from me and took two slow breaths. More calmly, he spoke again. "God will forgive me. The same way God will forgive my departed Amelia. You see, addiction is a disease of the mind. She did bad things to feed that disease, but she wasn't a bad person. I have a disease of the mind as well. I can't help but kill. I tried to exercise self-control, but my addiction eventually wins. I'm not going to hell for a faulty mind." Saris paused briefly. "I thought about suicide. But then I realized my killing did good in the world. The planet is overpopulated. The environment is stretched thin. We humans have burdened the land too much." He gave me a self-satisfied smile. "In fact, I'm going to turn this neighborhood, all 960 acres, into a reserve. It will increase the ecosystem of the State forest that adjoins the development's northern tier."

His rationalization of murder sent a shiver through me. It made me realize Lily wasn't his only victim. My daughter's death wasn't the first—or the last.

Reading my eyes, Saris confirmed my suspicion. "My father was my fourteenth victim. Well, by the hands of David. You see, Misty, David had worked for me for years. And then you took his life. I had to clean up the mess you made, and the body you left in the downstairs bathroom." Saris made a little gesture with his hand. "I tip my hat to you, Misty, for surviving a man who made his living by killing." Saris leaned back onto his elbows, sighed, and spoke in a dull monotone.

"Anyway, my father had to go. He was getting ready to sell all these lots. It's bad enough that paved roads cut through this beautiful property." Saris stopped talking for a moment while a sadness seemed to wash over him.

After a moment, a glimmer arose back into his eyes. His tone turned reflective. "I killed a prostitute myself when I was twenty-two. My first victim. After that I vowed to change my life, and it worked. Or it did up until David came into my life. That was ten years ago. Up until today, the prostitute was the only one I killed with my own hands. So I guess you and Tyler will be my second and third."

That last sentence shifted my attention away from my shock at hearing Saris recall his numerous murders and rationale for them. Now, a renewed concern about Tyler welled up within me. I wanted to ask him about Tyler but feared that was a banned subject. I gave a quick glance to the alarm clock on the nightstand, whose blue display read 10:28 p.m. *OK, I've only been out for about three hours.* Saris had said he intended to kill me in the morning. I might just escape between now and then. I just needed him not to change his mind and do it sooner. Regretting that I had provoked him, I suppressed my anger. "I'm sorry. You're right. I agree: addiction is a hijacking of the mind. Why would your situation be any different? Also, I agree with you about this development. It should be turned into a reserve. I love nature, Saris, and you know this." I looked at him, waiting for a nod of agreement.

He didn't nod. Instead, his eyes stayed coldly fixed on my face. Like he was analyzing my motives.

Trying to sell my words, I went on, "I mean, I am mad at you about my daughter. Of course I am. But I get it now. Honestly, after everything I've suffered, I wouldn't mind if you killed me in the morning. When you knocked me unconscious with the hammer, I had a vision of Lily in heaven. I want to be with her." I said all this in the most convincing way I could.

Saris's face gave me hope that he had bought at least some of what I had said.

In truth, though, I didn't want to die. Especially not knowing Saris would still be alive. Much as I longed to be with Lily in the afterlife, that would be someday. But not today. Across from me sat unfinished business. Silently, for an indeterminate time, we looked at each other. Using only my eyes, I tried to express compassion towards him. Towards a serial killer.

Saris's intensity unlocked. I saw the muscles in his neck and shoulders relax. He reached over to the nightstand. I didn't realize how hulked up in a rage he still was from when he slapped me. Like he'd been on the verge of killing me since I tried to shame him about

Lily. All he had to do was reach over and snap my neck. From here forward, I knew I had to be smarter, but my mind was foggy.

He turned back to extend to me a sandwich on a plate.

"You must be hungry," he said, in the same gentle baritone voice he had used that morning. The voice that had aroused me so recently now repulsed me. I accepted the sandwich, though. My stomach was growling from hunger pains. The fogginess that kept my mind from focusing may have been due to lack of food. I hadn't eaten anything all day.

Minutes after scarfing the sandwich down, I became incredibly sleepy. The sleepiness started to overpower me. I looked over at Saris, in a full yawn, and understood that I'd been dosed. Concluding that he'd spiked my water with sleeping pills, I thought, *Son of a bitch*, but didn't say it aloud. No point riling him up again. I tried to summon some adrenaline to keep my eyes open. My mind spoke sternly and silently to me, *Lord knows what he'll do if you fall asleep. He could rape you, kill you now, or kill you as you're waking up.* My heart quickened, sending the necessary blood flow through my veins. A discrete panic set in. The will to live helped me stay alert, but I didn't know how long it would last. I had to think quickly, so I said, "Here's my plate, and thanks," and handed it to Saris. He reached back to put it on the nightstand. With his back turned, I hopped backwards off the bed. Once on my feet, I hoped to run, but he was too quick, blocking my path. The bathroom where we'd had sex this morning offered the only escape. To my relief, my fumbles above the door frame found the key and I spun into the bathroom. I almost crushed Saris's hand when I slammed the door, locking it just as he wiggled at the knob. *Whew.*

Relief gave way to worry when the numbness of sleep caught up with me again. The fogginess in my mind grew worse. I couldn't fight it. The heaviness of my body forced me to slump down onto the floor against the door. I whispered a prayer as I rested my head on the cold floor. "For Lily, help me get through this. Mom's here. I'm here." I couldn't keep my eyes open. Blackness reigned again.

I began to dream.

CHAPTER 12

The Dream

My feet involuntarily lifted me into a run. Running in the blackness left me with a fear of impacting something or someone lurking on the path. Shoulders hunched and body tensed as I ran. I wanted to stop, but had no control of my mind; my legs kept going. Specks of light appeared faintly in the distance. I broke into a full sprint as if an unknown force was pulling me towards the celestial objects. The light brightened, forming cracks across the black void in front of me. Illumination ate away at all that was dark, leaving behind a blinding whiteness. I was stopped as the light softened, and a clear daylight forest encircled me. The forest was lush—and familiar. A woman's voice echoed around me.

"Misty ... I will speak to you in your native tongue." Her voice bounced off the trees. A warmth surrounded me, and I felt safe. A tall Native American woman stepped out from one side of me. She was adorned in beautifully crafted garments and jewels. She appeared to be middle-aged, with soft eyes that I couldn't help but respect. Suddenly it didn't feel like a dream anymore. I reached out and touched the bark of a tree, its reality palpable to all my senses. The woods smelled of recent rain, and every breath relaxed my body and soul.

The Native woman pointed to our surroundings and spoke eloquently. "Beautiful, isn't it? This forest is the same neighborhood in which you now live. Only the time has changed. It is the summer of 1589. We're still in what you know as North Carolina, only before all that you know. I am also Misty, or 'Light Rain' in our tongue, which can be translated into 'mist.' I have been appointed co-guardian over these lands, but I share that duty with an evil counterpart. I try to appeal to people's good nature in keeping these lands unspoiled. My counterpart, on the other hand, appeals to people's evil nature. Her name is Dust, which is the closest in English to our word's meaning. We both protect these lands in our different ways, governed by rules of Mother Nature. The rules keep us both as equal powers."

Surreal as this was, I believed everything she was telling me. Something in my gut told me this was all real. Even wide awake, when I would go on my walks into these woods, I would feel a sense of a higher power at work. I thought it was God, as the Baptist Church had taught me. Maybe it was this, Mother Nature and her guardians. Or it could be both.

The Native lady who shared my name continued, her tone more somber now. "Saris, the man who is after you was molded as a young boy by Dust, my evil counterpart. His father, who owned these woods, had a house on the road. Saris, like most curious eleven-year-old boys, decided to explore these woods and got lost. In the scramble to find his way back home, Saris fell and bumped his head. He had a vision of Dust, much as you are seeing me now. Together, they made a pact. If she helped him find his path back home, then Saris had to protect these lands from chainsaws and bulldozers. He made the deal. Little did young Saris knew, Dust had planted a seed of evil within him. He was sent out into the world to do her bidding. At times, Saris successfully fought the evil, but other times not. I helped as much as I could, but Dust had gotten to him first. You see, in the beginning, Saris was innocent."

Stunned and saddened by these revelations, I couldn't stop the tear that dropped. The astonishment of it all kept more tears at bay. This Dust was controlling Saris's mind, I understood. For the first time, I spoke to this gentle presence that shares my name. "Why my daughter? Why my family? We didn't even live near this property," I asked softly.

The Native lady informed me, "As you already know, your husband Tyler was a real estate mogul. Part of his portfolio included thirty-three acres of land adjacent to this property."

When she said this, I remembered that he owned a large tract of land—but I didn't know where.

"Four years ago," I heard, "Tyler casually visited that property alone before his police shift started. He stopped by at dusk to consider its potential for a housing development. He started to daydream about building a home for your family on the same land. But while Tyler daydreamed, Dust got into his head. She steered him into the city to where Amelia awaited." The Native lady stopped to let me process what she had said.

It started to make sense to me. Nature had started this chain of events, or at least Nature's evil part, and her name is Dust. Tyler killed Amelia. Therefore Saris killed Lily. After our daughter was murdered,

Tyler did in fact donate some of his land as a nature reserve. I assumed Dust provoked all these killings because she wanted to keep the land pure. I had another question. "What is the name of that reserve?" The Native lady didn't answer. Instead, she gave me a look. And then I knew. "Lily Reserve" was its name. I would see the sign with her name carved into it when I would head to town. It stood about a half-mile down the main road from this development. At first, It brought forth beautiful memories of my daughter. But then it left me with an empty feeling because she was no longer here—no more memories to be made. So, I came to ignore the sign. I never imagined that it was actually named after her. I'd been living near my daughter's reserve this whole time, and despite all our bad times together, Tyler had never told me. *Did he hate me that much?*

My perplexity must have been obvious to the Native lady. She gave me the answer before I even asked the question.

"Dust had turned Tyler into an abusive, frightening husband. He ceased sharing any intimate details of his life with you, which meant he neglected to tell you about Lily Reserve. You know he blamed you for her death. That blame wouldn't have been there if it wasn't for Dust. He couldn't look at the events leading to your daughter's death logically. But two months ago, the spell Dust had him under lifted. Ever since, he's been wracked with guilt for the way he treated you."

It all rang true. This explained Tyler's sudden recent change of behavior. It explained why he'd become so abusive after Lily's death. Deep down, I'd known Tyler was a good man. My encounter with him today had confirmed that.

This left me with another question. "I hired David to kill Tyler but backed out. It took everything I had to tell David to stop—because I desperately wanted Tyler dead. Or I thought I did. Was that Dust getting into my mind?" I hoped for one answer, an answer that could quell some of my guilt, a thought that had haunted my sleeping patterns for a year: was there an evil within me that could emerge at any moment?

The Native lady responded in a soft reassurance, "Yes, Dust lodged herself into your mind as well. She tapped into the evil that lies within all human beings, but Misty, you successfully fought her off. That's a rarity. It is something to be proud of."

That answer lifted a weight off me. Like the Atlas figure that I'd used to kill David, a piece of the globe had broken off, but only a piece because I still couldn't yet stand up fully. I did wonder why Dust had continued her assault on us, even after Tyler put his land in a reserve. "It was almost three years ago, right after Lily died, when Tyler donated that land. So why would Dust keep tormenting us? Her goal was to save the land from development, right?"

The Native lady answered, "You are correct. She wanted the land to be left untouched. However, while Dust had Tyler under her spell, she planned a chain of events that would lead to you and Saris getting together. A chain of events that leads to tomorrow."

"What happens tomorrow?" I asked, full of dread.

The Native lady stepped forward and gazed at me in a more pressing manner. Though still soft, her tone became urgent. "Saris has been remodeling his church, getting it ready, so to speak. Tomorrow he will preach to the largest congregation he ever had. Possibly over six hundred souls."

I was conscious that I was breathing heavily; I knew where the Native lady was going with this.

"He's going to kill them," she confirmed, "with a toxic chemical he plans to release into the church. The deaths will include himself. Dust can impose population control measures in the name of stopping environmental degradation. Saris is her puppet, and we need to cut the strings. This is why I came to you while you slept. You need to save them. Save them all. Several children will be present."

"I will, I will. But how?" I asked.

"That I cannot help you with, other than this warning. And to tell you that you have a fifty-fifty chance of survival. Mother Nature bars me from interfering unless your odds dip below that fifty-fifty chance. Saris will attack you early in the morning, and you will have to be ready. Once he is certain you are dead, he will head to the church. So stay alive as long as you can." The Native lady stepped closer, lifted my hand into hers, and squeezed it tightly. Her touch calmed and relaxed me.

Then, confiding one last detail, she said, "I'm sorry I was not able to stop Lily's death. I tried to get into Saris and David's heads to stop them, but I could not. Dust had full power over them. Today, after Dust sent that bear that you called 'Ralph' after you, I could then interfere."

Dust instructed Ralph to attack us?

She answered my thought, "Right. Both of us can use all living things as vessels for our plans. Since Dust used that bear, I had the power to help you and Tyler earlier tonight. I helped you two gain another chance." Finally, with a meaningful nod, the Native lady pointed at my stomach.

Instantly, I asked, "I'm pregnant?"

She nodded a yes.

I rubbed my stomach, noting that this dream had put me in a flowing white dress. Hope for the future resonated within me. This explained the sudden sex drive Tyler and I had shared in the depths of the woods while trying to escape Saris's wrath. Feeling hopeful, I asked one more question. "When I wake up, how will I know this is more than a dream?"

The Native lady's face seemed to shimmer as she answered. "Look for the blooming lily."

I happily accepted that sign.

Still gripping my hand, she spoke like these would be her final words to me. "Before I wake you, remember you're strong. Dust got to you once, when you hired David to kill Tyler. Remember: the first day you moved into this land was the first day you wanted him dead. You were supposed to let David kill Tyler. However, your good side won out in the end. That was your first victory over Dust. Don't let it be the last. Remain strong, Misty."

With that last sentence, the volume of her voice faded away. A swirling vortex of leaves encapsulated the Native lady, and blackness eroded the lush green forest.

Chapter 13

The Fire

I blinked into awakening. The cold floor stuck to my cheek. With a moan, I came back to reality. I was startled by a devilish eye glaring at me through the half-inch opening under the bathroom door. It was Saris, who had been watching me as I slept. I jumped up.

"Good morning." Saris's cheerful voice vibrated through the door. Hearing that cold baritone sound woke me fully. Through the bathroom window, I could see it was still dark outside. It must have been late; the glow of the moon was gone, sunken beyond the trees. I reckoned it had to be sometime before 6:30, when the sun rises that time of year. I wasn't sure how long I'd slept, but I guessed several hours. The sound of Saris shuffling behind the door sparked me to action. I tried to open the window, but couldn't budge it. As I struggled with it, the corner of my eye caught something white outside.

My vision zeroed in through the darkness onto a bright white lily. It was nestled between two shrubs across the road. The flower seemed to glow. My mouth dropped open with a gasp. My dream had, in fact, been a reality.

"Misty," an angelic voice called from behind me. I turned and recognized the Native lady's face. It shone, lifelike, in the heart of a metal cross that hung on the wall. This image felt more like a dream than my dream had.

She assured me, "You're not dreaming, Misty."

"How can I tell?"

"I showed you the lily. Wasn't that enough?"

Why the question? She knew I needed more proof. I couldn't harbor any secrets from her. Then I realized she wanted me to have some faith. Faith in the whole thing: we're at the whim of Mother Nature, controlled by forces of good and evil. That I could buy, had already bought, but these forces had been given names: Mist and Dust. These forces had killed my daughter. They had turned Tyler and me against each other, playing with my life, destroying it. If we are at the mercy of Mother Nature, I had to wonder, why keep going? Why bother? I felt defeated.

Mist interrupted this. "Since the beginning, humans have always been at the mercy of Mother Mature environmentally. But when it comes to free will, each person has it in varying degrees. Like the body's muscles, your free will has to be exercised to strengthen it. That's the human counter to nature's mental forces. There are complicated lines that neither Dust nor I can cross to infiltrate that free will. None of that changes the fact that you have every right to be angry. The scales of fairness are tipped against you, and it's because of Dust's enormous power. She's become the world's third most powerful co-guardian of a territory. She has surpassed the evil co-guardian of the suicide forest in Japan."

I remembered an employee telling me about this forest, how something about it encourages someone in it to take their life.

"Her strength also strengthens me as well, so a balance can exist. That's why I'm able to come to you in your dreams, and now into your real world. Remember, I fostered your reunification with Tyler. That gave you a second chance, and that's incredibly real!"

I glanced at my stomach and felt Tyler's life-creating seed inside me. Conjuring up the euphoric pinnacle Tyler and I had reached just hours ago, I shivered from the memory. The force that had re-stoked our attraction for each other, pulling us back together, must have been some external factor, I realized. I couldn't pinpoint it to the Mother Nature world but I suddenly and absolutely believed Mist now. I had faith.

"Look in the drawer," Mist said.

I opened the drawer beside the sink and found a small Bible. Then I realized what Mist had done; she had given me proof. Proof I wasn't dreaming. I studied dreams as a pastime, and my research had told me most people couldn't read when they're dreaming. I was one of those people.

I opened the Bible and read,

"In the beginning God created the heaven and the earth. And the earth was without form, and void; and darkness was upon the face of the deep. And the Spirit of God moved upon the face of the waters. And God said, Let there be light: and there was light."

I stopped reading, once again feeling the slow hum of the trains rumbling through me. I could feel a weight on me this time, like the statue of Atlas, but it wasn't the world that I held up; it was 600 people and their lives. All will be taken away by Saris and Dust, and only I could save them. Responsibility was nothing new in my life. For fifteen years, when I owned the diner, I'd had fifteen employees, and their livelihoods depended upon me. Every decision I made had affected not only me but their lives as well. But the weight I felt now was magnitudes greater than that.

Mist sounded off, "Hurry, Misty, before Saris kills those people." Immediately after she reminded me of my mission, her face disappeared. I had completely forgotten about Saris out there. I wondered if he had heard all that. I could see movement under the door, light dancing around his shadow. He seemed to be preoccupied with packing or something. I gazed at the floor, and at that moment, I enlisted myself in the fight to save the churchgoers. My first obvious directive: I had to figure a way out of this bathroom. I was sick of bathrooms; too much had happened in them since yesterday morning. Then I realized Mist had left me with a clue to get out. The three-foot silver cross that shimmered against the wall could bust that stubborn window. Each time I'd been in that room it always stood out to me.

Lifting the heavy cross off its nails proved difficult. Its weight caused me to stagger backward, and while trying to get a steady grip, I could hear Saris through the door.

"Goodbye, Misty." His voice trailed behind him.

I rested the heavy cross on the floor. "Please don't go." I was trying to stall him, keep him from leaving.

After a brief silence, footsteps approached the door. I saw shadows again through the crack. Waiting for him to talk seemed to take forever. Then he spoke like he was under a spell. "You know."

So I asked, "Know what?"

Again, a forever pause. I was about to give up waiting for an answer I already knew when he spoke.

"I have to kill those people today. Each of them will contribute to the degradation of the environment."

I responded sympathetically to appeal to his better nature. "No, you don't, Saris. They are innocent." I tried to reason with him. "Instead, do a sermon on how we should be better stewards of God's planet. Influence people with words. You're great at that." Still holding the heavy cross, I gently leaned it against the wall, approached the door, and pleaded, "Please, Saris. You're not this man. Children will be there." I put my hand on the door, sensing he was doing the same thing on the other side. Without him speaking, I felt a sense of compassion pass through the door. Then a cold, invisible malevolence struck my hand, and I jerked back away from the door.

The evil part of Saris spoke. "Last night, in my dreams, Dust told me you would try to stop me. She said the only way to stop you was to burn you up in this house. The fire would spread throughout this street. As you know, Misty, fire is good for a forest; it allows a rebirth, a cleansing." He stopped speaking and his shadow disappeared.

"Wait," I said. Remembering a paper on population growth that I'd written in high school, I tried to appeal to his logic. "You're doing the opposite if you want to control the population by killing all those people." The sound of his footsteps told me he had stopped; he was still in the bedroom. Hurriedly, I tried to make my case. "The 600 or so you'll kill will affect at least 3,000 people, assuming each person has five people who love them dearly. These individuals affected by this loss will find themselves with a void in their life. In most cases, these people will turn to having children to fill that void. That's why countries affected by terrorism, war, or low life expectancy have higher birth rates." I finished by saying, "You're doing the opposite, Saris. You're making it worse."

Saris chuckled. "You don't think we already figured that?" When he said, "we," I assumed that included Dust. "The people that will be in my church today are mostly complete families and friends. The outward birth effect will be zero. In fact," he added, "some close friends could commit suicide. Every person that will be in those pews has been carefully chosen for the greatest impact."

I felt helpless. I couldn't get into his mind. Dust had too much control.

The sound of his breathing reminded me he still stood behind the door. Breaking the pause, he said, "So I'll say again: Goodbye, Misty. Enjoy the fire."

I flung back a response. "If you start a fire, your parishioners will see it. Your church sits at the edge of this land. They will see the smoke; they'll leave before you even start your Sunday morning service." As soon as I said that, I thought, *Maybe I shouldn't have said that; the fire could deter people from attending church. And attending their deaths.*

Then I heard a haunting laugh from right behind me. *Someone's in here with me!* The villainous image of a woman appeared peripherally at my sight. Slowly I turned to fully encounter the evil.

Like a big TV screen, the oversized bathroom mirror displayed Dust's reddish face, black eyes, and long hair, black with gray streaks. Her face took up almost the entirety of the glass.

Dust's voice resounded like an echo chamber. "Hello, Misty. I can answer your question. As you burn up in this house, I will hide the smoke trails behind the clouds. Saris's unsuspecting parishioners will remain unsuspecting parishioners. They will happily enter the Evergreen Baptist Church—for the last time. Oh, to be sure, my counterpart Mist will provide the necessary rains to stop the fire, but not before it engulfs both houses on this street." Dust emitted a nasty chuckle. "By the way, Tyler is handcuffed to his bed. He will also burn up."

I started to say something in the way of a negotiation to stop the slaughter of innocent churchgoers, but Dust's image had vanished from the mirror.

Tyler's alive! Maybe I could save him, too. *I need to get out of this bathroom.* Perhaps I could just go out the door now. I leaned against the door to listen. Was Saris still out there? Was he dousing the place with gasoline? My attention was caught by a red flicker of light in the silver cross that I had leaned against the wall. It was a reflection of something outside. I looked out the window to see the bright white lily caught in a tiny tornado of fire. The flame streaked the lily's white petals; no smoke billowed from the supernatural fire. Abruptly, the torrent of flames stopped, leaving a little heap of smokeless ashes.

I leaned my head against the cold window with a new kind of sadness. The white lily had represented my daughter, and I felt her loss fresh in me. Blinking away tears, I looked toward the dawning sunlight draped over the tree line, with fading stars overhead. A low rumble startled me, and I turned to face the bathroom door. The rushing hiss and slight whistle of a fire starting sped me to act. I seized the two arms of the silver cross leaning against the wall. Smoke drifted through the half-inch opening in the door, confirming what I already knew: the house was on fire. I needed to get out. I knew I couldn't escape by the door because I could hear the blaze on the other side already tearing through the master bedroom. Time didn't allow me to hassle with an attempt to open the window, so I made a plan to break the glass.

I lifted the heavy cross, both hands gripped tightly around the base. I vibrated under the weight and intentionally dropped it against the window. Shattered glass bounced back at my exposed skin, its stings eating at my body. *Shit! I'm still in my bra and underwear.* I laid the corner of the cross on the windowsill and swiped its base along the frame, breaking up and removing the pieces of glass that still clung. Propping the cross against the window, I attended to the small cuts that dotted my body. A few tiny slivers of glass had punctured my skin, and I delicately picked them out. Luckily no wounds were too deep, only spots of blood that dried fast.

I snatched my bathrobe from the towel bar and swathed it around my body; I should have done this before I smashed the window. Barefoot, I carefully stepped around the fractured glass and leaned my head out the window. Damn Saris's tall house with his high ceilings. I searched for loose nails like I'd found in the other second-floor bathroom. I decided: *I'm going to lower myself out again.* Hopefully, not by my bra this time.

At first glance, I didn't see any loose nails. I pulled my head back into the smoke that was starting to filter into the bathroom. I found a long towel. Thankfully, Saris liked big towels. Flashes of flame already sparkled around the door. I had no more time to spare. Coughing my way back to the window, I stepped on glass, cutting my feet. I leaned again out the window, gasping, praying for something like a nail that I could hang this towel from. Jumping might kill me or break my legs, but given the rapidly approaching fire, I considered trying it without anything to slow my jump. Suddenly the house shook violently. The explosion nearly bounced me out the window. Then I noticed the siding outside the window had pushed out a nail. When the shaking stopped, the nail protruded just enough.

I smiled at the Native lady's helping hand. It had to be her; it was too coincidental. I needed a nail to get out, and she had provided one. Leaning over, I snagged the heavy cotton on the nail, folded it, and pierced it again. I picked away the remaining glass along the bottom of the window to allow my legs to safely swing over. I sat down on the windowsill and swung my legs over. Clutching the towel with both hands, I tugged at my improvised rope to test its integrity. It held tight. I was positioned and ready to jump when another explosion occurred. The house erupted below me in a cloud of fire, leaving behind a sea of burning grass. The ground I had almost leaped onto was blanketed in yellow flames, leaving me perched on the second-floor windowsill with no way down.

Swiveling around, I peered through the dense smoke filling in the bathroom and saw the blaze swallowing the door. Trapped, halfway out the window, I couldn't think about anything but all those parishioners who were about to die. They were just waking up in their warm beds, on what would be their last morning alive. They would get into their cars and head to what they considered a sanctuary. But instead of finding safety, they would enter the holy place to die. And I couldn't save them! *I need to warn them! I need to stop Saris!* Over 600 Lilys would die, and just like my daughter, I couldn't save them.

The fire closed in.

CHAPTER 14

Mists

Smoke came at me from all directions. The house shifted under me as the inferno grew. Mist had told me I had a fifty percent chance of survival. I guess the odds favored death. I was going to burn up alive or die from smoke inhalation; the thought pressed me more heavily than the figure of the hunched man with the world on his shoulders. Atlas had saved me yesterday morning. I need something to save me now. The house shifted downward again. I was about to collapse into the fire.

A breeze, maybe sent by an invisible hand, tilted my chin to look back inside. Through the smoke I could see the shower, the one Saris and I had had sex in yesterday morning. Somehow I knew the Native lady was giving me a way out, but I wasn't sure how the shower would help me escape the inferno engulfing the house. With no alternative, I left the window and stowed myself in the shower.

Sitting in the bathtub, I realized I would rather drown than burn up. I concluded that Mist was offering me a better death. Accepting my fate, I plugged the drain and, doubting the water would even work, turned on the shower. To my surprise, water sprayed out of the three-headed nozzle, briefly pushing away the choking smoke. I lay back into the rising water. In these last moments, I tried but failed to drum up memories of my daughter. Instead, I couldn't think about anything but the pipes in the house and how they were still holding up.

Then I remembered having passed the house when it was under construction. I'd noticing the bright copper piping springing out from the ground; now I assumed they would hold up longer in a fire. That memory gave me an idea. I sprang up out of the shower and to the "his and her" sinks, turning all the taps on full blast. I was enlisting fire's enemy—water. The water quickly overflowed and began to spill onto the floor. The tub behind me started to overflow as well. Maybe, just maybe, I could slow or stop this fire from the inside. Meanwhile, the bathrobe, now soaking wet, would help protect me from the flames.

Dark smoke outside caught my attention. I sloshed through the accumulated water on the floor and looked out to see that the lawn sprinkler system was misting water across the charred lawn, suppressing the grass fire. My moment had come. Wasting no time, I lifted myself onto the window ledge to jump, but the entire house began to lean forward. I slid back off the ledge and below the window for fear of falling out. A thunder like noise roared in my ears as the house gave way. I hunched down, one side pressed against the wall, my head pulled tightly against my knees. The floor below me splintered across some jagged objects before slamming onto something solid. With the water all spilled away, the floor rapidly got hot. I jumped up to see bathroom ceiling gone, and smoke rising where the roof had been.

The morning sun lit up the mist and smoke floating around me. Burning pieces of the house lay scattered on the lawn. It took a second for my mind to register that I was standing in what had once been the front yard, with remnants of the bathroom all around me. Saris's house continued to burn, but the front half of the second floor had collapsed into the yard, carrying me safely down with it.

I took a deep breath. I was alive! And now I could carry out my mission.

Seizing the chance I'd been given, I ran off onto the street, full of gritty determination. *Tyler and churchgoers, I'm coming for you!* The debris that littered the pavement didn't slow down my bare feet. A storm must have come through the previous night; fallen leaves, pinecones, and small branches lay strewn everywhere. Morning dew glistened on the roadside grass that led to my house, where Tyler lay handcuffed.

Was he awake, fighting to free himself? Or was he still unconscious from the hammer that Saris had so viciously swung into his head? One thing I did know: he wasn't free. Dust had told me he would burn up, and I believed her. I had to save him. But I hoped that saving him didn't mean I couldn't save the churchgoers. I persuaded myself that I had time; it was still early. *I can do it. I can save them all.*

Suddenly, from the woods ahead, I heard growling. At first, I thought the three animals that bounded into the street in front of me were dogs. Then I recognized them as adult red wolves, blocking my path. I stopped dead in my tracks. This was Dust's doing. Coming to grips with this obstacle, I warned myself that the short trip to Tyler and then the mile to the church would be fraught with danger. I was still at the mercy of those fifty-fifty odds. I couldn't claim victory until I made it to the church.

I faced the drooling beasts, which snarled, revealing their fangs. The standoff began; meanwhile the wind was whipping behind me, pushing the fire from Saris's house into the woods and toward me. I could feel the heat of the advancing inferno behind me. A cloud drifted overhead, blocking the morning sun. I figured that was the cloud that would hide the smoke from the unsuspecting churchgoers; Dust's power again at work. She was leaving nothing to chance. Suddenly her wolves kicked their hind legs and raced towards me. The standoff ended.

I veered sharply off the street and jumped into the branches of a large tree. I pulled my body up, feeling a tooth raking across my heel. In the nick of time, I hauled my legs out of the animals' reach and found a place to rest on a branch high up enough from the hungry wolves. Snapping and howling, the wolves jumped and clawed at the tree trunk, trying to climb up after me. I positioned myself to kick them if somehow they succeeded in climbing. But that wasn't my only danger. The wind had swept the fire across the street, now consuming underbrush just a few feet away from me. Recognizing the oncoming danger, the wolves darted off deep into the forest.

Unlike wolves, fire can climb. Getting a firm grip on the branch, I gently lowered myself, bracing myself for a drop onto the ground; with a fresh gust of wind, the flames surrounded the base of the tree. It was too late to jump. The fire was already roasting my dangling feet; I couldn't lift them out of danger without weakening my hold on the branch. Desperately looking for a way out, I discovered that my branch extended close to another on a different tree whose base was still outside of the fire. *I can safely drop there!* I moved one hand over, a move toward saving Tyler and the churchgoers.

It was like traversing the side of the monkey bars in a school-yard playground. Hand over hand, I moved along the branch, hoping it would keep supporting my weight. As close to the end as I could get, I found a three-foot gap between the two branches. I looked down to see if I could drop yet, but the fire had spread to the ground below. Gripping the branch tightly with one hand, I swung out the other and managed to grab the other limb. Once both hands were on the new branch, I moved along it, monkey bar fashion, to the trunk and painfully slid down the rough bark. I stepped into the ever-spreading fire.

With my feet searing from the rising flames, I instinctively dropped and rolled over into a still-unburned stretch of forest floor until the heat dissipated. I examined my hurting feet, finding them only red, not melted, burnt flesh. I must have acted fast enough before the fire did serious damage.

The bathrobe, a charred, wet mess, had protected me. But now it just slowed me down. I slid out, leaving it on the ground. In a panic, I ran towards our house, expecting that something else would stop me from saving Tyler. In a moment, through the trees, I saw the house's gray brick walls, still untouched by the fire. I ran past the spot where Saris had hit me with the hammer, up the driveway where Tyler's patrol car sat, its passenger door still open. Through the garage door, I rushed into the house and immediately called, "Tyler! Tyler!"

Dust had told me that he was handcuffed to his bed. Powering my way up the stairs, I skipped steps, desperate to get to the bedroom before Dust stopped me in some way. I swung open the bedroom door and, in relief at seeing Tyler, I doubled over. Also, I needed to catch my breath. That short break ended when I remembered the fire was heading towards this house.

Tyler lay stretched out, asleep.

"Tyler!" I called again.

His eyelids danced, not awakening, but indicating a troubled dream, the product of a stressed mind. His breathing rose and fell like he was caught in a nightmare. The two pairs of handcuffs chaining him to the mahogany headboard had to be hell for a man who always sought control the way a man should. Worse yet was how Dust had amped up his need for control, making him lethal and abusive. I desperately wanted to free the love of my life and restore him to the control he rightfully deserved. I decided I didn't want to wake him until I had freed his hands. I fumbled through his pockets for a key, but realized that Saris would have taken his key ring when he cuffed him to the bed. *There has to be a spare,* I told myself. I turned the room over searching for it. *In his office,* I thought. *Look for the spare key in Tyler's office.*

Leaving him in the room was difficult, but I had no choice if I was going to unlock the cuffs. I burst into the office and fumbled through his desk drawers. Furiously ripping the room apart, I concluded this was a waste of time. If there was a spare, a part of me knew, Saris would have taken it, too. How could I get Tyler off that bed? Searching my memories for answers, I wondered, *We don't have an axe, do we?*

I had to wake him. *Two minds are better than one.*

Back in the bedroom, I shook his arms and shouted, "Tyler, wake up! Tyler, wake up!"

Still asleep, he muttered, "Run, Misty. Save them. Save them. You have to save them." His words came from a dream, but was it a warning I needed to heed? If so, I had to abandon Tyler to his fate; in this bed, he would surely burn up. The bedside clock read 7:44 a.m. I still had time. The first churchgoers wouldn't start arriving until right after 9 a.m. Sunday school started around 9:30. Saris held a pre-service, meant for the parents whose kids were in Sunday school, but other adults attended, too, attracted by his hypnotic sermons. Like an opening act for a rock concert. Except he was both the pre and main act. I assumed he would wait to strike until his church was packed for the 11 o'clock service. His weekly show would be the last show for those six hundred souls. The bedside clock now read 7:45 a.m. The internal hourglass had been flipped. The sand poured. I needed Tyler awake and off that bed. *Come on, mind. Think.*

Power tools, I need power tools. I hurried downstairs to the garage and found a battery-powered circular saw. *Fuck, yeah.* I squeezed the button; the whine of the saw working was music to my ears. That mahogany headboard didn't stand a chance now. But my self-assurance waned when I noticed the fire was rapidly coming up the street. I had to move fast. I couldn't get caught in another burning house.

I raced back to Tyler. The urgency was real. *Lives are at stake.* I needed my partner if we were to take down Saris. I wasted no time; the saw came alive and in seconds tore through one of the bedposts. That was a huge relief. I've never been lucky with things working correctly when I need them to. "One down, one more to go." I let out a breath, and heard the fire cracking outside in our yard and approaching the front door. I got to work on the other post, "Keep going. Keep going, keep going, done." The headboard fell away.

I lifted Tyler's hands off the stumps of the bedposts and yanked on his arms. "Tyler, wake up!" I yelled in his ear. "We have to go. Come on, wake up! Please, come on! Tyler!"

He showed no sign of waking or responding in any way. He remained in a deep state of sleep. I assumed Saris must have dosed him with something like he'd given me. Suddenly, downstairs, I heard the windows shattering, along with the familiar roar of a wind-driven blaze. Over 200 pounds of muscle lay limp on the bed. There was no way I could carry him out. *Do I have to abandon Tyler to save the churchgoers?* My window of opportunity to leave the burning house was closing.

Nobody could hear my scream. "Noooooooo!"

Chapter 15

Evergreen Baptist Church

Tabitha Dawkins did not want to attend church this morning. At sixteen, she felt she was too old to be grouped with the young ones for Sunday School. Since no other teenagers regularly attended Evergreen Baptist Church, she felt a bit outcast.

Her mother cried, "Help your sister, Tabitha. Today's a special day. You know Pastor Saris is going to unveil the newly remodeled church."

Tabitha was annoyed by her mother's cheerfulness this early in the morning. *I just want to crawl back in bed,* she thought.

Just then, Rose tiptoed into the room, her hair disheveled and a toothbrush hanging out of her mouth.

Tabitha smiled at her five-year-old sister; she hadn't even put her shoes on yet. Knowing Mom was minutes away from loading them in the SUV, Tabitha acted fast to get Rose dressed.

"Thanks, sis," Rose said, standing on tiptoes to kiss her sister.

Tabitha leaned down and turned her cheek to welcome the mushy kiss. "Any time, little one."

"How long before I'm tall as you?" Rose asked. Tabitha hated the reference to her height but knew the question was innocent. She teased back, "I don't know. Maybe tomorrow?"

"When I wake up tomorrow, I will be tall like you? That's tall!" Rose's eyes widened at the thought.

Mom summoned them. "Come on, kids."

Rose sprinted to the SUV, her carefully brushed auburn hair bounced along her shoulders.

Tabitha slunk behind her sister. Already at five feet, ten inches she was taller than anyone else her age. Even taller than her mother. Unwanted attention followed Tabitha wherever she went. Her introverted nature made the stares and whispers unpleasant. Though she wore her ashy blonde hair pulled tightly back in a ponytail, sometimes she wished she could hide behind it. She often did try to hide herself in a room, steering clear of being the first to enter or leave.

Quickly passing out of town, the SUV cruised down the road through the woods. Tabitha always wondered why their church was out in the middle of nowhere. That bothered her mainly because no food options were nearby. Every Sunday as they left church, her stomach would growl the whole twenty minutes back home. *Why am I so hungry after church?* Tabitha wondered. Then she remembered the half-eaten cereal she left in the sink every Sunday morning. She was never hungry first thing in the morning. During the tedious ride, Tabitha plotted, *Somehow, I have to stow away a snack in here.* That would be a challenge; Mom seldom kept snacks in the house.

The tires crunched on the gravel as the SUV pulled onto the parking lot. The two-story church sprawled over its wooded setting like a modern fortress. Gray brick ran up to the tower where, just below the steeple, a circular window with bright white trim was set into the masonry. Tall windows lined both sides of the building, each letting light into both floors. Flowering shrubs surrounded the whole building.

Stepping out onto the gravel, Tabitha noticed an ominous cloud drifting in the woods beyond the church. It didn't seem natural to her, *But what do I know about clouds?*

In the imposing building's grand entrance stood Pastor Saris. Tabitha noticed a faraway look in his eyes, but her thoughts were interrupted by her mother gushing as she came up the walk to the front steps.

"Beautiful, just beautiful, Saris. Church looks amazing!" She rambled on, acknowledging the pressure-washed brick, freshly painted trim, and elaborate landscaping. Mrs. Dawkins couldn't hide her eagerness to see the inside.

Tabitha glanced at her dad, noting the buried jealously she'd come to know so well, resting just behind his green eyes.

Just about every Sunday, her mother flirted with the preacher. She always made an effort to speak to Saris and engage him in conversation as long as possible. Tabitha disliked this overt display, especially when her mother found a way to touch the pastor. She would usually offer a fake laugh to one of his jokes, followed by a gentle nudge of his shoulder; then her hand would slide down his arm.

Dad discreetly squirmed whenever he saw the two of them at this, but Tabitha always noticed. She always loved her dad but more so on Sundays.

Two more cars pulled into the parking lot as Tabitha walked down the flower-lined walkway and up the steps. As he always did, Saris greeted them as they entered. Tabitha shook his hand.

"Good morning, Tabitha."

"Good day, Preacher Saris," Tabitha replied, as Mom had coached her. She noticed something odd. Just before passing through the double doors, she saw Saris lean out and peer toward a broad grassy field that extended to the edge of the woods. He let a distressing look spill across his face. This puzzled Tabitha. He must have seen some kind of wildlife, she speculated. *Eww! Could it have been a bear?* Given how remote the church was, a bear wasn't out of the question, she knew. But once the family was all the way inside, her attention turned to her mom's exaggerated awe at the newly redecorated space. Tabitha rolled her eyes and forget Saris's look of distress.

The next ten minutes were filled with arrivals, mostly families who had kids young enough to attend Sunday school. Tabitha left her mother and father to find the classroom. She wanted to find a seat in a corner; Rose softly gripped her tall sister's dress with one hand and tagged along in a skip to keep up. The girls were turning to go into the classroom when an unseen boy called.

"Hey, Tabitha," his voice broke.

Tabitha found him in the classroom's far corner. She immediately recognized Logan from high school. With some embarrassment, she remembered how he'd approached her in the hallway two weeks ago.

Holding up a fist, he'd proclaimed, "Here's to tall people."

Tabitha had reciprocated, with her fist touching his: "Tall people!" she'd said, trying to sound confident, but a moment later she had tucked her head down in a blush. She thought Logan was cute. He had chocolate eyes and a surfer tan that naturally gleamed on him. His sideward glance as he walked away that day had made Tabitha think he felt the same way. With his back to her, he'd pushed back his wavy brown hair, and the motion drew up the sleeve of his T-shirt, uncovering his bicep. Something about that little gesture made Tabitha flush, almost giddy.

Every school day since, she would scour the halls between second and third period until he appeared, capturing her attention with her eyes studying him when no one was looking. It was the small things that kept Logan in her looking glass: from when he deeply inhaled, puffing out his taut upper body, and the follow-up gulp that protruded his Adam's apple under a strong jawline, to the tight shirts that he wore, always freshly washed and maybe even ironed. Unlike most boys in her school, his clothes weren't wrinkled or thrown together. He had a level of preppy—along with an edginess—about him. When he spoke, it was almost always with a smile, but underneath, Tabitha detected an anger in his voice. Not a dangerous anger, but an anger at injustice, like something bad had happened to him. *Or is happening to him?*

Tabitha knew she couldn't find out what it was until she simply stopped viewing him from afar and introduced herself, but she was too bashful ever to bring herself to talk to him. It was from a friend's shout that Tabitha had even discovered his name: "Logan." A quick search on social media revealed that he was one grade above her. On one platform, she found they had mutual friends and began to write a message to him. But losing her nerve, she backspaced, erasing the words. As the days went by, she longed to talk to him. The only words he had ever said to her was, "Here's to tall people." Until now, when he said, "Hey, Tabitha."

He knows my name, Tabitha happily recognized. She let him know she knew his, too. Her voice broke as she said, "Hey, Logan."

Logan stood in a gentlemanly manner, and offered seats to Tabitha and Rose. He towered over the corner of the low-ceilinged room at just over six feet, tall for a seventeen-year-old. Usually, when Tabitha would see a cute boy, she would hunch her body, trying to make herself look shorter, but Logan made her stand straight, proud of her size.

She found a seat at the back of the classroom, but left one chair between them. She didn't want to seem too eager to sit directly next to him. *Why is Logan here?* Tabitha wondered, nevertheless feeling ecstatic that he was. She hid her enthusiasm by delving into the Bible she pulled out of a cubby in the desk in front of her. Tabitha checked to see Rose was sitting with proper posture, obediently waiting for class to start. Tabitha smiled at the cute calm of her little sister, sitting behind a desk she could barely see over.

Rose's calm broke when others her age began to pour into the classroom. She bolted out of her seat to play with her peers. The room erupted into chaos, with kids running around screeching and laughing. Tabitha had fixed her eyes on her Bible, allowing herself occasional motherly glances at Rose, while still acutely aware of Logan's presence. In the corner of her eye, she saw Logan leaning over to tell her something. Mentally preparing herself for a conversation with him, Tabitha was startled to hear Miss Diana's voice as the teacher entered the room.

"OK, everyone, to your seats! Everyone ready for Sunday school?"

The kids responded in unison, "Yes, Miss Diana." Everyone rushed to their seats. Logan leaned back into his chair.

Diana announced, "Today, I'm happy to say, my son Logan joins us."

He wiggled his fingers in a child-like wave to the room full of kids.

They responded almost in unison, some saying, "Hello, Logan," while others said, "Hey, Logan."

While Logan smiled, Tabitha briefly got lost in his pearly white teeth and accentuated dimples. If every Sunday were spent with Logan, she decided, she would wake up in the same cheerful mood as her mother. *But for me to focus on a boy in Sunday school,* she told herself, *was something innocent.* Mom, on the other hand, was borderline cheating on Dad. Tabitha quickly assessed the difference between them. She didn't want guilt to tarnish her crush on Logan; being shy and socially awkward had already hindered her from starting a conversation with him.

Tabitha pulled her gaze away from Logan as Miss Diana beckoned her to come over to help pass out worksheets. These were for little children, not intended for someone Tabitha's age. Since she was usually older than anyone else in the class, Tabitha was accustomed to acting as Miss Diana's assistant, working one-on-one with the kids. This worksheet illustrated the story of Jonah and the whale. The kids were tasked with answering easy questions about the story and then coloring in an outlined whale, Jonah, and the sea. Tabitha got to work, helping the youngest ones come up with answers, noticing their eagerness to skip the writing and get to the coloring.

While busy helping Chad, a six-year-old who Rose played with every Sunday, Tabitha took note that Logan was helping Rose right beside her.

Logan handed Rose a box of crayons and pronounced, "Congratulations! You have all the answers right! Now you can color."

Rose swung her legs in excitement under the oversized desk and said, "Thanks furr helping me, Logan!"

Logan leaned over to Tabitha, flashed that grin that highlighted his dimples, and said, "Your sister's cute." He dropped his smile, but the light of that smile lingered in his eyes when he added, "So are you!"

Instantly, Tabitha felt herself blushing. Her breathing quickened. To disguise the undeniable attraction she felt for Logan, she rebuffed him. "Thanks, but I'm busy." No sooner had she spoken than Tabitha regretted it. She had come across colder than she'd meant to.

Defensively, Logan pulled back.

To redeem herself, Tabitha hastened to say, "I'm sorry. Thanks for the compliment. Truly! I didn't sleep well last night, so I'm a little punchy." Working up her courage, she let out a breath, grinned, and said, "I think you're cute, too." Chad and his worksheet forgotten, she let herself get lost in Logan's eyes. He seemed to find it just as difficult to look away.

An abrupt thud against the classroom window broke their lovestruck stare.

Rose squealed with fear.

Tabitha instinctively reached for her sister and stood up. Rose curled into her arms and buried her face in her shoulder. Silence fell over the room as everyone came to grips with the sight: a bloodied hand slowly slid down the window. Streaked blood followed the path of the hand, which squeaked along the glass. Near the bottom of the window, the hand curled into a fist and fell out of sight. Right before it disappeared, the bloodied hand had seemed to lose the life attached to it.

CHAPTER 16
The Tree of Life

If Tyler were afflicted by pain, maybe he would wake up, I reasoned. I rolled up his sleeve to expose his upper arm. For half a second, I considered using the power saw to slice his skin, but gave up on that idea. I didn't need to wake him up, just to go into shock from his injury. On the dresser, I found a pair of scissors.

Downstairs, the fire crackled through our life's possessions. Sheer anger quickened my pulse, knowing Lily's cherished possessions would vanish into the blaze. Fed up with our enemy Dust, my pure motivation to win brought the scissors against Tyler's skin. I held on to the conviction that good would win out over evil, all the while Tyler's blood oozed out and ran down his arm. I withdrew the sharp points and watched his face contort as he came to.

Pain worked. *He's waking up.* Proud of my improvisation in this dire circumstance, I dropped the scissors and ran to the bathroom. I found some gauze and wrapped it around the wound I inflicted.

Groggily, Tyler reached out and touched my face. "Misty, you're alive."

"Yes, I am, babe, and so are you! We have to go; we have to get out of here."

He raised his head, taking in the sound of the fire downstairs. Awareness of this new danger flickered in his eyes. He jolted off the bed, frozen on his feet, holding out his hand to maintain his balance, dizzy from standing up so quickly.

Impatiently, I allowed him a moment to gather himself. He steadied himself with a hand on my bare shoulder, reminding me that I was wearing only a bra and panties. Tyler ripped one of his white dress shirts off a hanger and pulled my arms through it. It hung just below my ass. He tried to button me but was moving too slowly. I took over.

Suddenly, something made me curious. A bandage was wrapped around Tyler's head, hiding the wound where Saris hit him with the hammer. Why had Saris bandaged him? And why had he been cuffed to this bed? I dropped those questions with a thankful thought: *I'm glad he's alive.*

Tyler draped his arm over my shoulder, letting me support his weight; he could barely walk yet. I led him out of the room, to see if getting downstairs was plausible. Turning the corner confirmed that the fire was raging, approaching the bedroom. Luckily the second floor of this house wasn't as high as Saris's.

I pointed to the windows. "We have to jump."

Tyler nodded, apprehensive but in agreement. He staggered to the window. Yanked it open, and did his best to lift me onto the ledge.

I was about to jump when he said, "Hang on. Let me lower you so the impact isn't so bad on your feet." I didn't want him to do that, weak as he was from being drugged.

I jumped before he could grab me. The ground stung my feet but not as badly as my first jump yesterday. I looked up; Tyler was leaning out the window.

"Are you OK?" he shouted.

I understood the urgency we faced, knowing Dust could easily send those wolves again. I urged Tyler, "Yes, I'm fine. Jump, babe; we have to get moving, but be careful!" By now, smoke was rolling into the backyard around both sides of the house. I stepped back, waiting for Tyler to jump.

In the window, he began to sway like he was about to pass out.

"Tyler! Stay with me!" I screeched. He slumped backward inside the house and out of my sight.

In a panic, I squawked, "Tyler! Wake up!" I tore at the grass for rocks and threw them through the window, hoping enough would pelt him to wake him up. The window remained vacant with no sign of movement beyond. In agony, I bent over and prayed to God and the Native lady for help.

I collapsed into a crying fit, unable to control the strings of saliva yo-yoing out of my mouth, hyperventilating at the morbid fact that he was about to burn up in this house, and there was nothing I could do about it. He didn't even know he was going to be a father again. I'd never gotten the chance to tell him.

Gasping for breath, still bent over, I heard a soft thud, then gentle footsteps. I looked up to see Tyler coming to my side. He had jumped. Tears of relief washed away my grief.

Tyler lifted me off the ground, enfolding me in a hug, and my arms wrapped around his neck. I rested my head on his shoulders, sniffling back the remnants of my crying.

His warm voice whispered in my ear, "Let's save them. I saw you in a dream. Only it wasn't a dream. You were speaking to a Native American lady who shares your name. I know everything now, and I know you're stronger than all of us. The evil Dust never got to you, the way she got to Saris. And to me."

Softly, I asked, "You know everything?"

He lowered me to my feet and gently glided his hand down my stomach. When he spoke, I could feel the immense love behind his words. "I have two things to live for."

I hugged him again, my face pressed into his chest. *He knows I'm pregnant!*

A deep boom startled us both. An explosion somewhere in the house blasted flames out the windows, snapping me back into a sense of urgency. I withdrew from Tyler's embrace. "We have to save the churchgoers."

"I know," Tyler said. "Saris will kill them all if we don't get there and stop it."

He really did know everything. He must have had a similar dream to mine. I wanted to ask him about the details, about what he thought of Mist, but we had a mission to accomplish. Our eyes linked, taking in each other, soaking up the last still moment. Then in synchrony, we broke the stillness and ran toward the street. Tyler's patrol car was on fire in the driveway, so we had no choice but to run. We turned toward Evergreen Baptist Church. We did not need words. I knew he loved me, and I loved him. We were in this together.

"Together" was the operative word. On the street, I glanced back at our house, crumbling into ash, seemingly being swallowed up by hell.

We picked up the pace, as fast as the injuries and the drugs let us go. Suddenly, I smelled fresh rain. Looking back, I saw a wall of water extinguishing the fire. It all came from one cloud that hovered like a UFO, unleashing the elixir of life on earth. As Dust had foretold, Mist would put out the flames but not before they had engulfed both houses. I just hoped that meant we were done with fire. Three times being almost burned alive? That was enough for today.

As I ran, I realized my legs weren't bothering me as much as they had yesterday. They emitted only a faint stinging sensation; the bandages Saris had applied held up well. Motivation to save the churchgoers propelled me forward.

With every ten feet of street I left behind, I remembered other things that motivated me before Lily died. When I'd first started the Diner, it was all about making money. Once that goal was satisfied around year ten, and after Lily's eighth birthday, I'd wanted to become more of a positive force for good in society. Even more so for my daughter's future. It had given me much pride to maintain fifteen good-paying jobs in my community. I'd felt I was nurturing the economy in my little way. As I ran, I reflected with appreciation on all the grueling, unforgiving work because the nuances of multitasking and the competition of owning a restaurant had forced me to grow both intelligence and willpower. Because I'd had to endure a lot each day with only a few hours of sleep each night, I grew accustomed to difficulty and hardship. Eventually, I even thrived on it, whereas most people would crumble and give up. In subtle ways, those hellish days had given me a skill that once again, this horrible weekend, was coming in handy. I have a feeling that will to persevere will help my chances for success in stopping Saris. But I warned myself: *I can't get too cocky.*

Pop! My insides felt the sound, deep and loud like a close lightning strike. I stopped. *See, I can't get too cocky.* A crackling noise pointed my eyes to a large tree that was tilting towards the street. As it fell onto the pavement in front of us, the tree came alive with indistinguishable movements along its branches. As it crashed to a stop, I heard the hissing sounds and noticed the tongues tasting the air; snakes were slithering off the tree and onto the street. Tyler held out his arm out to push me back. The reptiles were all moving toward us, and fast. Backing up from this latest peril, we had to analyze our next move, fully aware of Dust's effort to stop us from getting to the church. Tyler scanned the woods, searching for an easy path around the fallen tree. He let out a hesitant breath, which I understood to mean there was no telling what dangers awaited, whether deep in the forest or even along its edge.

The roadblock of tree and snakes left us no choice but to head into the woods. Tyler led the way, but before we even entered the forest, a red wolf stepped out of the shadows, blocking our path. I recognized the wolf from the pack that chased me up the tree earlier. It didn't growl but threatened us with a glare. The animal tensed its body, poised to run after us if we got any closer. Turning around quickly, we crossed the road and came face to face with another of the wolves.

Tyler's battle-ready posture made me nudge him back away from the animal. Grabbing his arm, I shouted, "No, Tyler, don't!"

He ignored me, broke my hold, and charged at the wolf. It jumped onto him, snapping its teeth, within an inch from his face. Tyler had enough strength to throw the wolf into the mass of snakes. They struck at it multiple times before it stumbled away from the venomous swirl. Tyler extended a hand, a signal for me to run with him, not giving the wolf a chance to attack us again. I raced after him into the forest. The trees swayed to an unfelt wind high above. Not putting anything past Dust's power, I waited for the forest to collapse on us, but we managed to get back to the road beyond the snake-infested tree. We ran, and we ran, never looking back to any danger that might have followed.

The church steeple finally appeared above the tree line, looming taller with each step. Tyler and I kept pace side by side in our final sprint to our goal.

As we drew closer, we were facing a side wall of the imposing structure. Around the corner, at the front doors, I could see Saris greeting a young girl. Before she entered the church *to die.* I wanted to yell and warn the girl but feared that would put her in immediate danger. Instead, we veered off the road into a field of waist-high grass that surrounded the church. Slowing to a stalk and lowering ourselves in the grass, Tyler and I exchanged glances to confirm our unspoken mission: to sneak up on Saris. Maybe, I hoped, Tyler could get him in a chokehold.

We went deep into the field, hoping the building would block Saris's view of our position. Suddenly, a loud wind whipped around us, highlighting our location. *Dust again!* The abrupt gust turned Saris's head quickly towards the field. He looked directly at us. Knowing him as I did, I could imagine the vile intensity with which his blue eyes must have dilated at the sight of us. Tyler and I stopped, dropping ourselves in the grass, a move that was too late. I sat up just enough to see if Saris was coming after us.

A car door slammed, and I could see Saris return his attention to greeting his arriving congregation.

I whispered to Tyler, "Should we make a scene?"

"No!" Pointing at Saris, he said, "Look."

At first, I didn't see anything out of the ordinary. Then I noticed his hand tapping the back of his suit jacket. The outline of a gun appeared, either in his back pocket or on a belt. His threat, clearly meant for us to see left me puzzled at how to stop him. I looked at Tyler and whispered, "You don't happen to have a gun on you? Do you?"

He shook his head, confirming the disappointing answer I already knew. Saris would have taken his police-issued gun, just like he'd taken his keys. And we had been too busy trying to get out of a burning house to load up on any other weapons. Then a realization hit me. A rear entrance opened into the church's central sanctuary. The door opened in front of the pews, right behind the piano. I pointed the way and whispered to Tyler. "The back door. We'll go in through the back door and see if we can somehow lock Saris out. We'll have to act fast while he's still busy talking to his arrivals."

With a nod, Tyler silently accepted my plan and broke into a crouching run through the tall grass. Following him toward the back of the church, I spotted movement in the grass. I seized Tyler's hand. "We have to move. The wolves are back!"

The words had scarcely come out of my mouth, when Tyler went down, the wolf on top snarling, and that was all I managed to see before I was startled by another ferocious beast jumping at me. I locked my arms over my chest, which knocked the wolf back for a split second. Before I could run, it caught my hand between its jaws. In anguish as its teeth penetrated my skin, I stomped and kicked at the wolf's body.

I managed somehow to get my foot on its neck and it unlocked its jaws' grip on my hand. Its growls dwindled to squeals as I pressed my foot deeper into its neck, finally cutting off any noise. Now the red wolf was struggling for survival. I looked into the animal's eyes to see a puppy innocence overtaking the wolf's evil glare. I was grappling with a real animal, native to these forests. Dust hadn't conjured up some supernatural entities to attack us; she was using real animals just like she had used us. She had appealed to the evil within each of the animals that attacked us, from "Ralph" the bear yesterday to today's snakes and wolves. Sympathy began to overpower me, and I slowly released my foot from the wolf's throat.

I put my fear aside, deciding I couldn't kill this animal. I stepped back, waiting for it to charge at me again, but the wolf jumped up and ran away. To my side, I saw the other wolf leaping away, too. I cried out, "Tyler! Are you OK?"

I got no response. The red-stained grass danced in the wind over where he should be lying. Alarm rang through my mind as I made my way to him.

CHAPTER 17

The Bloodied Hand

Tabitha held her sister tightly in her arms. The trail of blood in the center of the classroom's wide-spanning window gleamed luridly in the sunlight. Questions swirled in her mind. *Whose bloodied hand was that? Is it someone I know? Is there a murderer out there?* She looked outside into the field of sunlit grass to see if she could see anything else. The meadow appeared calm, with the exception of the wind, which sent ripples through the tall grass. No one dared approach to see the body attached to the hand. It was clear to everyone, even the children, that a life had been lost. Fear kept everyone far away from the bloodstained glass. Tabitha developed a sinking feeling about her parents. She headed for the door, Logan by her side.

Miss Diana was ahead of them. "OK, kids, let's go find your parents. Don't look at the window." Her voice shook. Everyone remained eerily quiet as Miss Diana opened the classroom door. As she peered out, a chorus of squeaking noises erupted from the hallway, frightening everyone. The door suddenly slammed shut from the outside. The impact pushed Miss Diana onto the floor; she slid across the hardwood, bumping into a desk. This time a few children began to cry.

From outside the door, a woman yelled indecipherable demands. Logan ran to his mother and reached out his hand. "Mom, here, take my hand. Are you OK?" His mother, a stunned glaze on her face, pulled herself up, helped by Logan's grip. She could utter only one word. "Bats."

"Bats?" Logan asked. "Who slammed the door? Mom?"

Not answering her son, Miss Diana staggered back to the door, tilted her ear against the wood, and pressed the weight of her body against it. Listening for the slightest squeak beyond the door, Miss Diana squeezed the handle, not to open it but to keep something—or someone—out. Tabitha and Logan knew it had to be more than bats that kept her barricaded at the door. First was the bloodied hand. And now this. It wasn't just Tabitha; she was sure Logan and Miss Diana also sensed they were under some kind of an attack. But from what?

Tabitha took charge with Rose in her arms and ordered the kids, "OK, listen up, everyone. Everything's going to be OK."

One kid cried, "I want my mommy."

Tabitha tried to console them. "Don't worry, guys. We will go find your mommies and daddies once Miss Diana knows for sure the hall is clear of bats. In the meantime, let's all line up against the wall here." The kids obediently formed a line, with some sniffling and wiping teary eyes. Tabitha succeeded in calming the frightened children. The room grew quiet. Everyone listened intently for any noises, familiar or unfamiliar. Huddled against the wall with the kids and Logan, Tabitha's impatience moved her to act. She lowered Rose to the floor and whispered, "Stay here, Rose."

"Where are you going?" Rose's fear of being abandoned rang through that question.

Tabitha squatted to face her little sister. She pushed Rose's hair behind her ear and assured her, "I'm not going anywhere. I'm just going to look out the window."

Rose pursed her lips in a pout but relaxed enough to lean back against the wall.

Tabitha stood up and turned toward the bloody window.

"Tabitha, what are you doing?" Logan asked.

"I have to see what's going on."

Logan stood close by his mom, his chocolate eyes wide.

Miss Diana gazed at Tabitha, silently imploring her to be careful.

Tabitha stepped cautiously toward a solution to the mystery: who did that bloodied hand belong to?

Inching closer to the bloodstained glass, the first thing she saw was a pair of men's dress shoes lying in the green grass, and after another inch forward, a pair of black dress pants. All of a sudden, a swirling, black, shape-shifting cloud appeared through the window. Tabitha froze. Zeroing in on the unnaturally fast-moving cloud, she realized it was a flock of bats. They were headed straight for the window. Keeping her eyes on the bats, she backed up against a wall. Rose wrapped her tiny arms around Tabitha's leg.

Everyone squealed and cringed at the sight. Dread filled Tabitha. Could the window withstand the impact of so many flying bodies?

Miss Diana, still holding the door, began to murmur a prayer.

The first bat struck the window with a thud. Then hundreds slapped against the glass. A long crack formed.

Miss Diana twisted the knob, attempting to open the door. She turned to Logan and Tabitha. "The door is locked from the outside. We're stuck in this room." Swallowing hard, Miss Diana slid down the door. Huddled on the floor, she retreated into a mumbled prayer, ignoring pleas from her son.

"Mom, get up! We have to do something."

Oblivious, Miss Diana rocked herself out of reality, repeating over and over, "Deliver us from evil."

Standing over his mother, Logan checked the door himself. It didn't budge. He banged his fist against it, yelling, "Help! Help! Anyone out there!"

Beyond the door, a heavy wind whistled like a blizzard, as if a cold, barren land and not the Evergreen Baptist Church's hallway lay on the other side.

Trying to stave off the rising panic, Tabitha motioned the kids to hunker down on the floor. Keeping her voice as calm and soothing as she could manage, she said, "Everyone cover your heads. Between your knees." Pleased to see the kids following her orders with little fuss, she added, "Good job, everybody."

She turned to Logan, hoping he could help come up with a plan. He'd given up on trying to open the door. What sounded like a winter storm still blasted through the hallway. Instead of acknowledging Tabitha, he stared at the swarming bats. She got lost with him, staring at the bats smacking, then flying away from the window. *Maybe they're flying away,* she let herself hope. But the black flock circled back, walloping the glass with their bodies again, all at once.

Some hit the window so hard they fell to their deaths. Another crack formed. She feared this odd behavior would repeat itself until the inevitable happened: the window would shatter, admitting a swarm of bats determined to—do what? Tabitha's dread grew as she remembered that bats often carry rabies.

Then the third flood of bats hit the glass. Cracks spread across the glass like spiderwebs. Then the classroom's freshly painted walls gave Tabitha an idea. Earlier, she had noticed a roll of blue painter's tape; she rushed to get it and ripped off long pieces. Desperately, she hoped the tape might hold the glass together. At least this could buy some time until help arrived, Tabitha reasoned. With urgent precision, it took just a few seconds to cover the cracks; then she began to unwind the tape all the way across the large window.

Smack! Again the bats hit the window, putting a tremendous strain on the glass. Tabitha jerked back, fearing the worst.

Logan dashed to a work table, flipped the table over and tugged at a leg. His muscles strained with each twist and turn until the table leg gave way into his hands. He held the wooden leg like a baseball bat, his boyish innocence instantly disappearing.

Tabitha saw a man, ready to fight. Then she noticed Rose huddled on the floor, her head between her knees, the other children whimpering around her. She knew then she had to fight for her sister, who couldn't. Tabitha went for a table leg of her own; knowing she didn't have the strength to wrestle it off with her hands, she kicked at it.

Logan tapped her on the shoulder. "Here, take mine," he said, offering her his weapon.

Tabitha took it with a quick, "Thanks."

Logan went back to work, breaking off a second table leg. Both were ready to play baseball with the bats. But just as they assumed their fighting stance, they noticed the bats were no longer smacking the window. They had scattered, flying away from someone fanning something at them.

Tabitha recognized the person outside. "Dad!" she exclaimed, surprised but hopeful. Then an uneasy feeling sank into the pit of her stomach. Dad was out there, alone, fighting off hundreds of bats.

CHAPTER 18

Cross to Stab

Tyler's fretful eyes met mine. Both his hands pressed against a gash along the side of his abdomen. Blood seeped over his fingers. I leaned into the imprint Tyler made in the grass. I wanted to help but hovered over him, my hands extended, unsure on what I could do. For some reason, I focused on the black uniform shoes he'd been wearing since yesterday. Fresh tears cooled my heated face. I was losing the man that I loved.

A hinge squeaked and the back door to the church opened, just a few feet away.

I sank further into the grass, pressing my fingers against Tyler's lips. Then I remembered the gun that Saris had tapped as a warning to us. Unable to run, I looked at Tyler. We stood no chance against bullets. I couldn't see, but I felt the enemy was near. It was clear what I had to do. I had to change my position from prey to predator. Saris wasn't going to find us. I was going to find him. I mouthed to Tyler, "I love you."

He shook his head and tried to sit up and stop me, but the pain of the wolf's bite had paralyzed him.

Stealthily, I lifted my head above the grass.

I felt the wind as a bullet whizzed by my head, but heard nothing. The gunfire had been silenced; Saris was now at point-blank range.

I leapt toward Saris and rammed my body into his. He fell back onto church's back steps. I heard the gun clatter onto the concrete. Like a cougar, I pounced and tore at him, not giving him any time to react. I ripped the large gold cross off his neck and stabbed him with it, repeatedly. Sprinkles of his blood spritzed onto my arm.

Amid my stabbing frenzy, someone touched my leg. It was Tyler.

I stopped.

Tyler had seized Saris's gun and was holding it at his face.

I jumped up, dropping the bloodied cross.

Saris put up his hands and tried to defend himself. "I have to do this, guys. Dust is not wrong. People are destroying this planet! Killing these people will help others have a better life. Have you asked yourselves what Mist will do to fix the environment? Mist and her kind are the reason why we have legalized abortion. That's evil within itself."

I barked back, "Saris, if you think abortion is evil or wrong, think about what you're planning to do now! You're aborting 600 people."

Saris lowered his hands in front of him, and a flash of reason appeared in his eyes.

I continued, "Don't you see? We can fix this climate crisis without lives lost."

Saris seemed to take to heart what I was saying.

I appealed to him further, "If Mist is the reason why abortion happens more frequently than it should; if she manipulated women into making a difficult choice and that choice didn't come entirely from them—like being brainwashed into a decision—then Mist is wrong. You know my stance on this issue. I've been caught between the pro-life and pro-choice arguments my entire adult life. We talked about this, Saris." I looked over at Tyler, one hand on his wound, and the other holding the gun at Saris. I could tell he was displeased that I had referred to a conversation with Saris when we were together. I looked back at Saris and concluded, "Let the people behind you go, and together we'll find a better way to help the environment."

Saris looked at both Tyler and me and said, "You don't understand. Mother Nature has been manipulating humans since we became self-aware two hundred thousand years ago. It's been the constant push and pull of both sides. Depending on the side you're on, you view the other as evil. That's why in this country, we have Democrats versus Republicans. Both are wrong if they get one hundred percent of what they want. Both are right if they get near fifty percent of what they stand for. It's a balance."

I couldn't argue with that. I agreed with Saris that a balanced society is a better society. That's why I'm a swing voter during elections. But that didn't explain what was happening today. I still couldn't understand why he thought the 600 people entering his church today had to die for the environment's sake. More than seven billion people inhabit the planet. Why all this fight to kill 600? So I questioned him.

"Saris, why are these 600 people so important to your crusade to save the planet? How are their deaths going to make a difference? Don't tell me it's population control; 600 is a drop in the bucket to 7.6 billion people."

Saris grinned the insidious grin I'd grown accustomed to in the past twenty-four hours. The light of reason had vanished from his eyes. He answered, obviously unafraid of me knowing the truth, "These people will be spreaders of death. They will be infected with a virus that will incubate in them for weeks, but they will be contagious the whole time. This virus will have a fifty percent kill rate. With half the human population wiped out, the environment can heal."

I thought back. Mist had said he would use a toxic chemical. She hadn't mentioned a virus. Was she wrong? Unless the virus was manmade. Maybe that's what she had meant by a chemical. Nonetheless, I felt misled about my mission. I thought all six hundred would die today. It was much worse than that. *Try a few billion deaths.* Also, could Saris have been right about Mist and abortions? I didn't have time to delve further into that train of thought. Therefore I asked one last question. "Are they already infected?"

"No. But the bats are in the room."

I knew then what he meant. Bats already had a bad reputation for spreading disease. Not just rabies; we all remembered the COVID-19 time so well. That virus had a roughly one percent kill rate. I couldn't imagine the world's reaction to something that would kill half of those infected.

On the steps to his own church, Saris relaxed, unfazed by the gun Tyler pointed at him. A weight seemed to lift off the preacher and settle onto me. *My part in the future of humanity just got bigger. A lot bigger.* I had always wanted to have a lasting, positive imprint on the world before I died. Well, I couldn't have been given a better chance to prove myself. As I took that in, the church was filling up, each person inside a "Patient Zero."

Between me and them, Saris sat in the way. But for the first time since I'd met him, Saris looked meager and weak. His elegant suit was disheveled and speckled with blood, and his hair, usually perfectly combed, was a mess, all thanks to my attack with his own cross. His blue eyes had lost the order I'd been so accustomed to. But despite all this, Saris spoke confidently. "You can go ahead and shoot me. It won't matter. You're too late. I have someone inside who will summon the bats if something happens to me. For maximum impact, I would rather infect all 600 I'm expecting today, but when it comes to viruses, you know as well as I do that one person infected is all I need. As far as I'm concerned, my mission in life is done."

Tyler and I looked at each other. I believed Saris. Tyler obviously did, too. It left us with a question: who is this person working with Saris? Do we have to kill him? Or her?

From around the church I heard still more cars pulling into the gravel parking lot. I inhaled an earthy scent the breeze was carrying from the forest. The forest was something worth fighting for, but not at the expense of half of the world's population. I looked back at Saris, smugly sitting on the steps, the church casting a dull shadow over a man who appeared to be already dead. I figured he wouldn't put up much of a fight if I ran past him and stormed into the church. I had taken one step to test his reaction when I heard people chattering through a frosted window nearby.

"Where's Preacher Saris?" his parishioners were asking.

Suddenly, Saris clutched his own throat. Blood poured over his fingers. All I heard behind me had been a soft puff. Turning, I saw Tyler lowering the gun with its silencer.

"Tyler, what did you do?"

His only answer was, "We have to evacuate that church, and Saris stands in the way."

He was right, of course, but I was angry. Angry that Saris couldn't be saved. My anger surprised me, because until moments before, I had wanted him dead, especially for Lily.

But he wasn't dead. Not yet. Saris staggered to his feet, a hand still clutched against his throat, and he looked me in the eyes. The fury in his face dissolved into a boyish pout. His blue eyes faded, and I could see an eleven-year-old boy in him as he stumbled helplessly across the grass.

A vision flashed behind my eyes: Saris at that age, *which Mist had told me about,* was lost and searching for a way back home. I could see young Saris running through the woods, crying out to his mother and father. He tripped and bumped his head on a rock and went into concussive sleep. The wind stirred the browning autumn leaves into a funnel from which Dust materialized. Ingrained forever in my mind were those black eyes. Her face shone red, as if a still flame rested just behind her skin. Dust leaned down and caressed the unconscious boy's cheeks. Despite this woman's menacing look, she expressed empathy for young Saris.

My vision broke with Tyler hissing, "Come on, Misty! What are you doing? We have to go inside."

Trancelike, I responded, "I'm coming." Sorrowfully, I watched as Saris's grip on his throat relaxed, allowing the blood to spill. He pressed his bloody hand upon one of the church's first-floor windows, and crumpled onto the ground.

To his death.

I wanted to believe that Saris finally found his way home in the afterlife, being embraced by his mother and father. I realized at that moment that I no longer held him responsible for Lily's death. Other forces had been at play, like Dust. She was my real enemy.

"OK," I said to myself, mustering up my courage for my next fight. But first, I insisted, "Hang on, Tyler. Before we go in, let me close that wound." Seeing the significant amount of blood that had dripped down his leg, I commanded, "Take off your shirt."

He struggled to get the white T-shirt over his head.

"Here, let me help." I pulled at the neck and ripped the cotton off into a long strip. Perfect. I carefully wrapped the cloth around his torso, tucking in various points to provide the necessary pressure to suppress the bleeding. I retied the bandage over the earlier wound I'd created on his upper arm.

Despite his blood loss, Tyler appeared to be doing better. No longer looking defeated, as he had earlier while lying in the grass.

I ran my fingers along his muscled arm and said, "You ready to keep the people away from those infected bats? And figure out who is this person helping Saris?"

Tyler flashed a smile, and I noted a healthy color returning to his face and chest, erasing the grim paleness. He leaned against me, his shiny brown eyes held mine. It felt like his gaze said a thousand words about how much he loved me. He concluded that love story with a kiss. The kiss lasted little longer than a quick peck but long enough to provide me with hope. The kind of hope you held about your future as a kid before the stark realities of life poisoned your optimism.

"Let's go," Tyler declared, storming up the steps. Tyler provided cover for me as we opened the back door to Evergreen Baptist Church.

CHAPTER 19

The Parents

T he sight of us, bloody, bandaged, and brandishing a gun, sent shrill screams echoing through the church.

We shouted, "Get out! It's not safe!" Tyler threatened the bewildered churchgoers with the gun.

Many of the people rushed out the front door, but about a dozen adults remained stunned in place.

Tyler yelled this time, "Get out, or you will die!"

One woman stammered, "We can't leave without our kids." A man nudged her, as if afraid that she had put the kids in danger just by announcing their presence. I recognized the antsy look on this man's face. It was the look of a parent with a child in danger. Everyone carried the same expression, like a hazard light had come on. The light kept flashing over and over behind their alarmed eyes.

Then it hit me: standing before me were mothers and fathers, all of them frightened. The parents' unsettled breathing drifted through the sky-high sanctuary until it was interrupted by a click.

My eyes followed the sound to an enormous clock, its hour hand showing 9:30 a.m.

The good news: church hadn't started, so everyone hadn't arrived. The bad news: Sunday school had already started, so kids were here. I assured the parents, "We just want everyone to evacuate. We're not here to hurt you in any way. Go get your kids and leave. Go home! And tell anyone you meet coming to stay away from this church."

Reluctantly, the parents obeyed, milling down the center aisle toward the hallway.

Cautiously, Tyler and I followed. He maintained the authoritative air he'd assumed when we came in. "Come on!" he urged people to hurry. His bare chest flexed as he commanded them.

Everyone's pace picked up. Meekly, a woman spoke up, "Where's Preacher Saris?" Her tone was passive, as if merely passing the time.

I didn't buy it. I could infer an agenda hidden in her voice. Was this Saris's helper? I knew I had to keep an eye on her.

"He's outside," I answered, leaving it vague and watching for any suspicious shift in her demeanor.

Her face remained stoic, devoid of emotion. Too devoid. She kept something carefully locked behind her sea-colored eyes—a secret.

Out of the sanctuary, we entered a hallway lined with snow-white doors. Perfectly aligned along silky brown painted walls, they gave the space a narrow feeling. I counted thirteen adults, not including Tyler and me, all couples except one. A younger man with fire-red hair stood alone. Could he be Saris's right-hand man? Was he headed for a door to open a room full of bats? I kept a close watch on him and the emotionless woman.

"Halt!" Tyler blurted.

Everyone stopped, startled.

Something thumped behind the double doors at the end of the hall. I watched the two brushed-nickel doorknobs, side by side. They didn't move. But then came another thump and then another. It became apparent, once we heard the high-frequency chirps, that I had guessed right. Bats were flying in that room. I signaled to Tyler, pointing at the cursive writing on a door closer to me. "Sunday School," it read, just one room away from the confined bats.

I paused, about to enter the classroom and get the children out, when a woman broke from the pack. Not the woman I had my eye on, but someone different. Her husband looked confused as she darted toward the double doors.

I shouted, "Tyler! Look!"

He pulled the trigger, twice. Blood sprang from her waist and her back, an avalanche of red flooded down her light-blue dress.

"Noooo! . . . Becky! . . ." Her husband wailed. The silent gunshots had knocked her to her knees, with one hand extended. She hit one of the handles before she collapsed and the door to the bat-filled room cracked open.

Everything paused.

Then hundreds of tiny flapping wings swooshed overhead. The door to the Sunday School classroom began to open, and I slammed my body against it to shut it. Whoever had tried to open it couldn't see me but had probably seen the bats. I kept my hand firmly on the doorknob, keeping the children locked in.

I screamed into the chaos, "Get those bats out of here! They're infected with a virus. Don't let them bite you! Someone go open the door to the sanctuary!"

Tyler nodded at my orders, and ran, hunched over, back up the hall. Overhead, the flock of bats seemed to follow him. A few parents dropped to the floor and huddled against the wall, covering their heads. The fire-red hair guy wiggled at the doorknob to another room. Locked, as I suspected.

Then I watched something disturbing happen. A bat would land on someone, nip or scratch them, and move on. The desperate swats from people were no match for the creatures. In moments, everyone but me had been attacked, and the flock streamed on over Tyler's head, like a black river floating in the air. Nature undoubtedly had intelligence today and was poised to win. Dust might already have won. Everyone was now infected, except me, and as far as I knew, Tyler.

Followed by the river of bats, Tyler disappeared into the sanctuary. The parents sat up to check the scratches and punctures the bats had left.

I listened for Tyler, terrified for his safety. The noise of the flapping swarm diminished into silence. He must have opened the back door to let them outside. I figured the bats would comply, fleeing from the church. After all, their job here was done. The virus had just crossed the species barrier.

It was disheartening to watch the parents losing something. An innocence about the way the world works dissipated in their eyes. The foreboding glances they directed at me made me realize: they knew a deadly pathogen now coursed through their bodies. They

had heard, and now believed, my cries. *"Get those bats out of here!*
They're infected with a virus. Don't let them bite you! Someone go open
the door in the sanctuary!" I felt I had lost this battle. Half of them
would die. I remembered Saris's words: the virus had a fifty percent
kill rate. Gulping back the tears, I was already mourning the loss of
these parents. *How long do they have?* I wondered.

Then I realized: there was no way in hell I could let them see
their kids behind this door I was holding. These parents could already
be contagious. They couldn't even go out into the world.

A heavy thought pressed down on me. *I have to forcibly quaran-*
tine these people. That amounted to kidnapping. I couldn't be responsible for almost four billion deaths. Like the Atlas figure, I could
truly feel the weight of the world on my shoulders. The responsibility
crushed me, leaving a nauseous, sickening feeling. This time I prayed,
not to Mother Nature, but to God.

Out of faith, a steely resolve surged within me. Metaphorically,
I lifted that globe off my shoulders and into my hands. "I've got you,
world," I muttered to myself. I wasn't going to lose this next battle.

The red-haired guy spoke. "OK, let's get our children out of
here." He aroused the group into full agreement. All stood up to
face me.

I was the only thing that blocked them from seeing their kids.
Now was the time to explain everything to these parents. I had to
do it quickly and convincingly. They would have a lot to digest. So
I spoke, firmly but softly. "Wait. We can't go in just yet. I have to
explain what this is all about. You've been—"

With a creak, a cool breeze pushed the half-opened double
doors wide open. More bats? Nope.

It was Dust.

Her human form took shape while a gale blew me back from the door that I held. The wind grew stronger and stronger. The pounding gusts forced me down onto the carpet. From the flabbergasted cries of the parents behind me, I could tell no one else could stand either. Actual dust blasting in my face made it difficult to see, but I made out Dust standing at the end of the hall, her lips pursed together, blowing. Her demonic face was awash with triumphant glee. She was pushing us out of the hallway, but why?

As I slid back, I tried to dig my fingers into the carpet's low pile. Where was Tyler through all this? I squinted, straining to see the Sunday School classroom door. I thought of the kids. Dust's motive became clear: she was keeping us away from that room. The children were in danger.

But the door wasn't the only entrance to the classroom; with that thought, I allowed the wind to toss me the length of the hall. I knew I had to go outside and enter through a window, and I had to act fast.

Pushed almost to the sanctuary doors, I was attempting to gain my balance and rise to my knees while the wind slapped my hair across my face. Something rolled onto my legs, pinning me in place. I couldn't move. I turned to see the woman Tyler had shot. Her lifeless body had been rolled down the hall and onto me. She had left a red path of blood on the carpet that led back to Dust.

I forced a stare at the malevolent spirit. Maybe I could read her or appeal to her with a look. Instead, her eyes, black as coal, fed on my hope. Eating away at it. I turned away before I lost all hope.

I strained until the dead woman slid off.

Someone grasped my hand and lifted me, pulling me at a run into the sanctuary. It was Tyler. To my delight, he was safe.

But looking around, I saw no one else. Feeling both relief and urgency, I asked him, "Where are the parents?"

By then, Tyler had led me out the back door where we had entered. All the parents had gotten out before us, and were throwing objects and swatting at the swarm of bats. A dad swung a broom back and forth over his head.

It took me a moment to process the scene. The bats were hurling themselves against a window, trying to enter the Sunday school classroom. Part of Dust's plot to infect the children, I presumed. Saris's body lay in the grass below the window. The woman with sea-colored eyes knelt beside him, wailing. Through the cracked glass, I could see a girl crying out to her dad. It was the same girl I'd seen enter the church earlier. Her dad was the man holding the broom.

"Stay back darling," the man insisted.

Shadows fell over me. I looked up into the sky. Dark clouds had rolled in. All at once, the bats scattered and flew away. I could feel someone's gentle eyes. I let the sensation guide my eyes to the grassy field. There she was—Mist. Here to save the day—I prayed.

Chapter 20
The Choice

A roaring noise turned my eyes back to the church, and to a tornado that had just appeared. Shingles peeled off the roof with ease and flew into the sky like birds. The funnel danced its way toward us. I turned back to Mist for guidance, and she pointed to an opening in the forest. I knew then that the tornado had come from her. It was her way of keeping the parents away from their kids. I found Tyler's hand. Shouting to be heard over the wind, which sounded like a freight train, I told the parents, "We have to follow the lady in the white dress! Trust me!"

Far deeper than any noise, I could feel the force of the spinning vortex not far behind. The ground shook, and I could barely stand as I took off, with Tyler in hand. Some of the parents, at least, were running with us. As if by some supernatural breath coming before the twister, the waist-high grass parted before me. A zig-zag pattern of parallel paths cut through the field, giving everyone an easy escape to where Mist awaited.

I looked back to see a mother braving the tornado. She couldn't—wouldn't—leave her child. Her husband screamed at her futilely as she approached the church's shattered window. The ferocious wind snatched up the woman and threw her into the field ahead of us. I ran to where she landed to find her lying still, her head twisted unnaturally. Her neck must have broken. Her eyes were still open wide with terror.

Without meaning to, I screamed.

Tyler calmed me with a comforting squeeze. It helped assuage my shock. His bare masculine warmth gave me some reassurance. I didn't think Mist would kill someone. I glanced down the field to see her beckoning with her hands, guiding the parents into the woods. Was she to be trusted? Was Saris right that she had her own sense of evil? She didn't seem to acknowledge me or this latest death.

I turned to see the tornado continuing its spinning rage, but not in any random way. No, the vortex kept going back and forth along a line that ran along the church's side, as if purposely blocking anyone from getting near the kids inside. With one last look at the dead mother, I reasoned that she was a casualty in a greater war. Sometimes someone has to die to save millions or even billions.

"I'm fine," I told Tyler. We headed toward Mist, this time at a walk.

Before we got to Mist, she started speaking to us. "The choice wasn't easy, but it was right. Right now, I know you're thinking I might harbor an evil side. It's true that my kind, the counter to Dust, sometimes has to kill," she confirmed, "but it's always for the greater good."

Tyler and I halted in front of her, where her caring eyes captivated me.

"Yes, sometimes I persuade women to get abortions, but it's not for the reasons you think. It's not for population control. It could be for a variety of reasons, not always black and white, whether it be an unfit mother or children with brain abnormalities that would make them a psychopath later in life. In the four hundred-plus years that I've occupied this region as the Good Mother Nature, I've only persuaded thirteen women to carry out abortions. That's out of the millions of pregnant women who have since lived in my domain and subject to my influence."

That confession still made me uneasy, but I believed her. Despite my misgivings, I knew Mist was someone to listen to and follow.

Tyler gazed in awe at the spiritual being before us, making me recognize he felt the same way.

She confessed something else with a sole focus on me. "I didn't want to mislead you about Saris's plans for today. But I did, slightly, because 600 deaths versus a few billion creates a greater weight. The obstacles you had to overcome to get here were enough pressure. In some form, Misty, you've always carried the world on your shoulders. I didn't want to break your back." Her eyes cast a motherly, protective shine on me that felt almost like a shield.

Mist stepped closer to us and said with more urgency, "Listen, you two, my powers are limited. I used most of them today with the tornado and all."

We looked across the large field at the dissipating funnel.

Her voice forced me back to her eyes. "Eleven of the parents are in a force field I created in the woods. I had to hypnotize them to walk toward it." Mist pointed between two large trees that gave way to dark green shadows of a lush forest. She looked back at us and said, "Two were killed. One by you, Tyler." She was referring to him shooting the woman who ran toward the door that held back the bats. "The other by me," she said, indicating the mother who lay in the field with her neck broken.

"Those remaining eleven, as you know, are infected with a very deadly and infectious virus. The parents cannot, I repeat, cannot enter society. They have to stay isolated in this forest for one month. That's when the virus will be fully out of their system." Her tone saddened. "Four to six of them will die from the virus. You'll be tempted to take them to a hospital, but that would be a grave mistake. Hospitals won't be able to save them anyway. It's up to the both of you to keep them in here. I don't have the time to explain it to them. You two are true believers. More than anyone, you understand the consequences." Mist inhaled and continued, her tone positive. "The good news: I was able to use my powers to make both of you survive the virus. You two will not die from it. However, you can spread the virus, so you will also need to quarantine in the woods. Just like the parents, for thirty days."

That took a weight off because I was worried about Tyler dying.

"But after today," Mist concluded, "I will not be able to help." She sounded like we would never see her again.

I quickly asked, "Why?"

Before Mist answered, she sighed, "I've used up all my powers, to the point of breaking the laws of Mother Nature. When I break the law, I'm dethroned and forced to go back to the other side."

Tyler asked, "What is the other side?"

Mist reached for both of our hands, and she held them together. Once again, her touch relaxed my body and soul. The sensation was stronger this time, and I figured it was because Tyler was here with me. Then something told me her next words would prove insightful, so I listened carefully as she answered Tyler's question.

"The other side is different for everyone. Heaven or Hell is based on you, and what you consider Heaven or Hell to be. I will be punished for breaking the laws of Mother Nature—but not forever. I will eventually enter my heaven."

Before she could say anything else, I interjected, "What about Dust? She's done a lot in the past two days to stop Tyler and me. Hasn't she used up all her powers?"

Mist's answer didn't disguise her disappointment. "No, Dust hasn't abused her powers. It's well within her right to use living things to get her way, from the bear and the wolves to the snakes and the bats. And even Saris. She could even use fire and lightning."

I had quick, disturbing flashbacks to every obstacle that Dust had thrown at me. I shook them off and asked about the last one. "What about wind? She blew the parents and me down the hall of the church."

"She can't use wind, other than to blow fire," Mist explained. Unashamed, she confessed, "That was me getting into Dust's mind. I'm not allowed to get into my counterpart's mind, nor is she allowed to get into mine. I broke the rules, and I used her to blow you and the parents down the hall because the parents were about to overpower you and enter the Sunday School classroom to see their kids. And infect them. Dust's presence was already nearby, in the room filled with bats, so I used her. The whole time, subconsciously, Dust knew I was lodged in her mind. That explains what happened when you were staring at her at the end of the hall; she tried to eat away at your soul and turn you to serve her. She obviously failed. In fact, Misty, Dust has always had trouble getting into your mind."

Mist paused enough for me to ponder that statement thoroughly; *"In fact, Misty, Dust always had trouble getting into your mind."* She had said that before like I'm unique, but I don't know what makes me different. What is it inside me that fights off Dust's mental game? What am I doing right? Or is my mind under Mist's control? If so, where's my individuality?

Mist resumed for what I expected to be answers, "Understand this, I can't get into your mind either because you have your own free will of good. People who are completely self-aware are impenetrable to our influence. That self-awareness can happen in the middle of our molding, and then we are blocked from the clay, the mind."

That's good, I thought; I have my individuality intact.

"Misty, you gained full self-awareness the day you decided not to have Tyler killed. Dust left your mind that day. However, self-awareness is not permanent, and it can be weakened with age, environmental factors, or with drug and alcohol abuse. You have to keep your mind sharp and logical. It requires discipline."

Mist fell silent; a slight smile illuminated her face.

Tyler and I briefly looked at each other. Our hands were still linked, still held by Mist. He stood tall, an alpha male with no inkling of disbelief in his shining brown eyes. I could tell he was waiting for something else from Mist.

I was, too. She hadn't told us everything, but I felt that she was about to.

And she did. "Once I found out who was going to replace me, I had no issue with breaking the rules. You see," she said, looking directly into my eyes, "I was mortal once. I died on these lands over four hundred years ago." Mist stopped, and from somewhere nearby, I could feel love within a familiar presence. She squeezed our hands, and her voice broke under suppressed happy tears. "My replacement . . . will be Lily."

I pulled my hand away and spun around, looking for my daughter. I didn't see her. I reached back and took Tyler's hand again. I could feel his racing pulse in his palms. That told me he felt the same desperate anticipation I did. We both wanted to see our daughter.

Mist stepped back, urgency in her voice. "You will see her throughout this journey, but at limited intervals. In a moment, you will have three minutes with her before you have to continue your mission. Once the three minutes are up, the parents will be waiting inside the force field I created. It will give way in fifteen minutes. In that time, you will have to convince them that their children's lives depend on following you. Then guide them to an abandoned house that lies hidden in the middle of this forest. Lily will show you how to get there."

Mist shifted her body and lowered her voice, now full of warning. "Dust will continue to try to stop you. Remember, she wants the world to be infected with this plague. Dust can and will get into the parents' minds. She will seek to persuade them either to flee or to kill you. Also, Dust still has the animals at her disposal. She will use them."

Her tone reassuring again, Mist went on, "Lily will help. After all, she's the new counter to Dust. She's the newest of the world's 333 good nature co-guardians. Yes, that means there are 666 in total, half of them evil co-guardians. In your world, that number is often associated with the devil or the sign of the beast. Our system partly influences that negative connotation because if either side breaks the balance, even the good, mayhem will fall upon the world. Lily's and Dust's domain consists of just over 3,000 square miles. It covers the same part of southeastern North Carolina that Dust and I held. That's the smallest area that any other guardian pair hold, but between them, Lily and Dust will be the world's most powerful. To put that in perspective, they will be a hundred times more powerful than the pair that cultivated and spread COVID-19 starting in 2019."

Once again, Mist looked deep into my eyes, but she did the same with Tyler, too. "Your Lily met all the qualifications to become my successor. One of which was that she died on this land."

That's something Tyler and I knew. Lily's body had been found about ten miles north of here.

"David brought her into these woods," Mist said. "She escaped him for almost a day, and was able to stay ahead of him for hours before he found her. You know the rest."

We did. Tyler and I knew the details from her autopsy all too well.

"The other qualifier," Mist added, "is that she's able to resist evil from entering her mind"—Mist looked directly at me—"just like her mother." Lily became self-aware weeks before she died. For someone her age that's quite a feat."

I stood awestruck, both by this revelation and from knowing I would see my daughter again. I had nothing to say.

Neither did Tyler.

Mist gulped, and in a sweet sorrow, said, "Goodbye, you two. The choice was easy. Lily will do more good than I did. She will be a powerful foe against Dust."

Loose leaves and grass spun up into a vortex that blanketed Mist. Abruptly the debris fell back down, leaving a sandy cloud that the sun illuminated. The eye-level cloud broke up slowly, and in it, I could make out my daughter. A joy I'd never felt before bubbled up inside.

Lily called out, "Mom, Dad!"

I ran to her.

CHAPTER 21

Goodbye

Tabitha ran to the cracked, half-taped-up window and cried out to her dad outside, "Dad! What's going on?"

Rose clung again to Tabitha's leg awaiting their dad's response.

"Stay back, darling," he warned.

Father and daughter looked at each other, the love from both still penetrating the distorted glass.

Then suddenly she heard what sounded like a plane about to crash into the church. The building began to vibrate and dirt pummeled the window as if sprayed by fire hoses. The flying soil blocked Tabitha's view of her dad, and her hope.

The fragile window shattered.

A glassy mixture of debris exploded across the room, pelting everyone. The tornado howled, muffling the children's screams.

Instinctively, Tabitha turned and fell to her knees. Scooping Rose against her stomach, she leaned over, wrapped her arms around her little sister, and created an enclave, protecting Rose from the flying objects.

The blast of wind through the window flung everything around, pushing against Tabitha's back. Desperately squeezing Rose, she thought of her dad outside, wracked with worry about his safety.

As suddenly as it had begun, the wind let up. The tornado moved away. What Tabitha heard now was the church's far side now taking the brunt of the ferocious vortex. Then, abruptly, the earsplitting storm stopped.

Occasional bits of debris plopped onto the ground outside. The children stopped screaming.

Logan interrupted the cautious silence, "Is everyone OK?"

Tabitha inspected Rose for cuts or scrapes.

"I'm OK," Rose said calmly.

That alleviated her big sister's distress. Tabitha turned her attention to Logan, crouching alongside his mom. Miss Diana's eyes were glazed, shock still etched on her face, and unresponsive. Tabitha knew then that she and Logan were the ones in charge.

Giving his mother a reassuring hug, Logan got to work checking on the kids, huddled along the classroom wall. Pieces of ceiling littered the desks that had slid across the room, acting as a cover for them. He moved the desks back, letting daylight touch the children. Everyone seemed unharmed, but they all peered up at Logan, helplessly waiting for guidance.

Tabitha went cautiously to the shattered window and scanned the field outside. The sun was back in full force. She squinted, looking for her father or mother. No sign of anyone. She reviewed the last few minutes shocking events: first, the bloodied hand, then the bats, and finally the tornado. It all left her with a multitude of questions, starting with: where did Mom and Dad go?

She noticed something in a corner. The body of preacher Saris had been blown into the classroom. It lay behind a file cabinet the wind had dislodged from its corner. From across the room, no one else could see him.

Unsettled as she was at the sight of Saris's dead body, the matter of finding her parents seized Tabitha's emotions at the moment. Turning away, she told Logan, "Let's get everyone out of here."

He must have seen a dreadful something in her eyes; he stepped across the room far enough to see the dress shoes sticking out from behind the cabinet. Before the kids or his mom became aware of the dead man, he urged her, "All right, Mom. Let's get up." He lifted her to her feet and, with Miss Diana limply propped up on her son's right arm, he opened the door into the hallway.

Tabitha silently mouthed, "Saris" and, with Rose at her side, stepped past him and into the hall.

Discreetly, Logan glanced back at the body he now understood had been his church's pastor.

Did Logan feel any sympathy for his death, Tabitha wondered. Just as she wondered, too: had Saris, somehow, deserved to die?

Tabitha's instincts told her the pastor's death was warranted. She had never trusted Saris. Maybe it was because she suspected a fling between him and her mother.

Tabitha shivered; the hallway had a chill. It gripped her more deeply when she saw another body, a woman this time. She lay at the end of the corridor, where it opened into the sanctuary. An irregular streak of blood extended the length of the hall.

"Who is that?" Rose asked innocently.

This alerted Tabitha that she had to shield her little sister's eyes from the sight. She didn't want Rose to see the blood or the body. "Don't look," she insisted, pressing Rose's head against her thigh.

Logan stepped up beside her. "It's Becky Jenkins."

Tabitha knew who that was. She remembered her as another of the little flock of women who'd been smitten by Saris's charms. That just worsened her fears about her own mother's fate. Might she have shared in some divine punishment for her web of whispered words and flirtations with Saris?

A moaning cry interrupted her thoughts. Tabitha and Logan turned to see the children had followed them into the hallway. All were on the verge of tears. Nine innocent souls, including Rose, saw Becky Jenkins dead. All but one. A boy named Chad had been behind them. He shot out between Logan and Tabitha, gushing, "Mom, Mom, Mom—"

Little Chad's mother lay dead in a puddle of blood.

Logan steadied his mother against the wall, chased after Chad and scooped him into his arms.

The boy thrashed about in Logan's arm, pounding him with his fists, wailing, "I want my mommy, mommy—" Still fighting, Chad got a good look over Logan's shoulder. Now he saw it. Death. The boy's mother's lifeless eyes were wide open. Even at six years old, Chad fully understood and collapsed into defeated sobs.

Logan hugged Chad like he never hugged anyone before, but unable to take away the hurt this little boy felt, all he could offer was a hug.

Motionless for a moment, sharing in Chad's grief, Tabitha looked up to see sunlight streaming into the sanctuary. She clung to a fleeting hope and asked herself, *Is this light a beacon to Mom and Dad?* With Rose's face still buried in her side, she hurried down the hall to investigate.

With a gesture to stop her, Logan wrestled off his dress jacket, still clinging to Chad.

Tabitha got his meaning, took the coat, and respectfully draped it over Becky, covering her face and staring eyes. Tabitha looked away, not wanting those eyes to haunt her later—like in her dreams.

Tabitha, Rose, and Logan—carrying Chad—stepped into the chapel. The other children followed, lined behind them like little ducklings. Miss Diana, back on her feet, came last, shuffling in a zombie-like trance. The light streaming into the sanctuary came through a hole the tornado had punched in the ceiling. It looked to Tabitha as if the heavens were shining into the church. She called, "Dad? Mom? Anyone?"

No reply.

Off in the distance, sirens sounded. Police were coming, probably ambulances, too.

Tabitha felt an urgent need to find her parents. "Look at me," she told Rose. "Stay with Logan. I'm going outside to find Mom and Dad."

Logan gave her a worried look. "I think we should wait for the police. We don't know what's going on. It could still be dangerous outside."

"I don't think the police are going to solve this," Tabitha replied. "I might not ever see my parents again. I have to try, Logan. I have to try and find them. Please, will you watch Rose?"

He held her eyes, disapproval in his glare, but nodded a reluctant *Yes*.

Tabitha dashed out the church's back door. Steam rising from wet grass as the sun drying it made it hard to see across the field. She called again, "Mom? Dad?"

She got a bad feeling about the waist-high grass, sensing that it harbored something. Then she heard a noise. A growl or groan from an animal. Or animals. She dived into the field, following what sounded like some creature eating. Heat and anxiety made her sweat as she frantically rushed toward what she expected to be a scene of horror. She could hear the sound of flesh being torn.

In desperation, Tabitha leaped over the grass until she saw what she had dreaded: three red wolves were noisily devouring a carcass. The victim was a woman. The frozen horror in the dead woman's eyes exploded Tabitha's terror. It wasn't her mother lying there, but that fact provided no comfort or relief. Tabitha had already seen three dead bodies in the last few minutes. That led her to an appalling rationale: that she would stumble upon two more dead bodies—and they would be her parents.

Tabitha wept. One of the wolves paused in its chewing to growl at her, but she scarcely noticed amid the stormy sea of worry crashing against her mind. Something glittering in the grass caught her attention. It was a necklace, a gold cross. She recognized the jewelry; it belonging to preacher Saris, who wore it every Sunday.

She swept it into her hands, shivering at the blood staining the tip. Tabitha couldn't drop it because it offered a clue. It appeared the cross had been used to stab someone. *Was this the murder weapon that killed Saris? Can't be,* She thought, *It would require too much stabbing. His hand was covered with—*

A hissing rattle erupted from the tall grass, making her leap back, but not quick enough. A bite struck her leg mid-jump; the rattlesnake clung to her as she fell, finally releasing its fangs and winding away. In agony, Tabitha felt the venom coursing through her. She clung to the bloody cross, her heart racing uncontrollably at the thought of dying. She just wanted to find her mom and dad. That's all she wanted.

Well aware of death knocking at her door, Tabitha struggled to her feet and staggered back to the church, abandoning the search for her parents. Looking for them would be pointless if she died in the attempt. First, she had to save herself. Hearing sirens now close by, pulling into the parking lot, Tabitha put her hopes that officers or EMTs would know how to save her.

She had almost made it to the church's back door when a bat swooped down from the sky, scratching her on the arm. Tabitha swatted frantically, but the flying disease vector had already flown away. Before she could even begin to calm herself from this attack, she spotted one of the red wolves at full charge toward her.

Snarling, the wolf clamped its teeth around her snake-bitten leg, jerked her off her feet and dragged her.

She screamed for help. Her backside burned from the friction as she was pulled across the rough ground. Before she knew it, she was halfway across the field and approaching the tree line. Her screams didn't let up. "Ah, no, help, no, no, no! Help!" She had never raised her voice so high in her sixteen years, and it finally hit its limit when it cracked. That moment of silence let her hear Logan. She realized he was behind her, chasing after them.

She managed one last cry, "Logan! Help!" The pain, the venom, and the inertia of being pulled so fast combined to make Tabitha incredibly dizzy. She had just seen the shade of trees overhead before passing out.

CHAPTER 22
The Catch

Logan stood over Tabitha, panting. He had never run so fast in his life. The wolf had left her here, deep in the forest. *But why?* he pondered. Logan took to inspecting her and saw that her leg was bleeding from the two punctures the canine's fangs had made. Then he zeroed in on another wound, two smaller bite marks near her ankle, a few inches down from the wolf's bite. He figured a snake had bitten her.

Based on hearsay about how to treat a snakebite, Logan thought he knew what to do. He unbuttoned his dress shirt and kneeled next to Tabitha. She was still unconscious but breathing. Still alive; Logan wanted to keep it that way.

Tabitha had put on a yellow dress that morning, and he lifted the hem over her knees. He tightly wrapped and tied his button-down around her thigh, to slow the spread of the venom. Logan leaned over, shook her shoulders and called, "Tabitha! Wake up!" But instead of coming to, her face remained placid, as if in a peaceful dream. Studying her face, Logan thought about how attractive she was but quickly expelled that notion from his mind. He felt creepy for thinking about such things during this peculiar and deadly Sunday. Logan pulled the yellow dress back down over her knees, removing any temptation for his mind to wander inappropriately.

He shifted his focus down her leg and wondered whether he should control the bleeding from the wolf bite. He thought he remembered something about bleeding out a snake's venom, but had no idea how much bloodletting was too much. He looked back at her face and was pleased to see her cheeks were still a healthy shade of pink. Still, he wanted to clean around the wound. Scanning around for a cloth of some kind, his eyes ended at his own chest.

Quickly, he took off his white undershirt and began to dab at the blood on Tabitha's skin. With every pulse, a small bubble of red would emerge. Logan let each drop soak into the tank top. He dabbed for several seconds until the white cotton turned crimson. Trusting his intuition, Logan knew it was time to stop the bleeding. He pressed the fabric against her leg and wrapped it up as a bandage.

Looking again at Tabitha's face, he silently pleaded, *Please, wake up.* Still kneeling, he leaned closer, hoping to see any movement, any sign of life, in her eyes and mouth. Gently, he said, "Tabitha, please wake up." He touched her smooth face, hoping to spark her back to awareness. But she kept an angelic stillness that frightened him. He wanted to yell for help but realized he was too far into the woods. The trees that surrounded him would muffle any cry, too far from any human to be heard. Also, he didn't want his voice to beckon the wolf back. So for now, he remained silent.

Logan questioned his abrupt feelings for Tabitha. He had only seen her twice in his life, yet he felt a strong desire to protect her. After all, he had run after her—even when it seemed like the wolf would never release its grip.

He wondered, would he have done that for anyone else? He could only think of his mom. Logan knew he had a selfish streak, which had brought him to church today. But was it pure attraction to Tabitha that had made him follow her into the forest? Or was he simply trying to save another human being in danger? The woods summoned a breeze but not an answer.

Kneeling and shirtless, Logan didn't know what to do next. The wind rippled his scanty chest hairs, raising goosebumps. It felt strange to be outdoors without a shirt, especially since he wasn't playing soccer. Logan had recently learned that he could garner a girl's attention just by taking off his shirt. On the field, he would catch a glimpse of girls checking him out as he played. Their obvious admiration gave him motivation and made him a better player.

He'd just turned seventeen, and relished the masculine appearance his body was transforming into; even his teammates and friends held newfound respect for him. Logan had always wanted control, in every aspect of the word. His childhood had been nothing but constant upheaval. With each decision Logan made, and each day older he grew, he was slowly getting a stronger grip onto his life.

Then today happened.

Logan shook his meandering thoughts and saw that a leaf had blown onto Tabitha's cheek. He removed it. Her lips were always naturally pressed together, like she was waiting for a kiss. It had been the first thing he'd noticed about her in school. Now he couldn't take his eyes off those lips. The story of Snow White scrolled through his mind. *Kiss her.*

Consent! She didn't give you consent! Those words flared out like a warning from the media, which after all had half raised him. He scoffed at the fragile generation to which he belonged. *Come on. One kiss. That's all, folks.*

Besides, Logan rationalized, she would wake up at the touch of his lips. He recognized the narcissism at play here, but that didn't stop him. The space between their faces narrowed. Logan's body grew hot. His closed mouth brushed against hers. That touch gave him courage; he pressed harder, his lips firmly against hers.

Tabitha quivered, her eyelids fluttering. It was like Logan had dreamed: his kiss had resuscitated her. Returned her to life.

She punched Logan hard in the nose.

"Ouch!" Still hovering over her, stunned, he didn't know what to say.

Tabitha pushed him away and sat up, amazed that he would try such a thing. The pain along her ass stung; her leg throbbed. "What are you doing?"

"You wouldn't wake up!" He yelled, releasing his grip on his nose and checking for blood in his palm. It came up dry.

Tabitha looked at his chest, in spite of herself. She was impressed by how defined and cut it was. "Why is your shirt off?"

"Look at your leg!"

She did. A tightness encircled her thigh. Lifting her dress, she saw that it was a shirt—Logan's, of course—tightly wrapped. *The snakebite.* She couldn't feel any sign of the poison anymore and concluded that Logan had probably saved her. Then she registered that another improvised bandage, blood-soaked, covered the wolf's bite. Suddenly it occurred to her: had it been the wolf that actually saved her? That its bite had allowed the tainted blood to spill instead of reaching her heart? But why would the wolf have dragged her in the first place? Maybe its bite could have drawn out the poisonous blood, but why would an animal save her? She was missing a piece of the puzzle. That bugged her.

Unwrapping the button-down Logan had tied around her thigh, Tabitha demanded, "What in the world is going on today? Has Mother Nature gone mad?"

Then, just like that, her anger vanished. She softened into the scared girl she was. Tears welled up and easily flowed. She whimpered, "Where's my mom and dad? Are they already dead?"

Logan, who a moment ago had looked so strong, now appeared helpless. He had no answers to console her with. Instead, with a look of determination, he swooped her into his arms.

Tabitha needed that hug. She shook in his embrace. Logan held on tight, enfolding her fear, and flexing his muscles, displaying his physical strength. This didn't seem like showing off; if he wanted her to feel safe, it was working. Tabitha gradually calmed down, soothed by Logan's squeezing warmth.

He offered reassuring words. "We will find out what is going on."

Feeling better, Tabitha withdrew herself from his bare chest, regretting that she no longer felt his heartbeat. She extended his navy blue dress shirt to him, a suggestion to get dressed again. She desperately wanted him to cover up, she admitted to herself, because his body was only a distraction. Admittedly, she'd never seen a guy who looked in such good shape as Logan did. Not in person, anyway. On a screen, they had all seemed airbrushed or faked. The reality of Logan and his body left Tabitha disoriented, unable to process all her emotions. It was like she was being pulled out of today's reality and sucked into a romance novel.

Now was not the time to explore some fantasy with Logan. Tabitha steeled herself to face the horror she knew was still in store. She implored him, "Put your shirt on."

Those dimples she'd always admired came back, along with a wicked smile. Tabitha didn't understand what was amusing him. She followed the direction of his eyes, which were casting a wayward glance at her torso. Tabitha looked down and saw her panties exposed. She realized, embarrassed, that she had lifted her dress too far to unwrap his shirt from her thigh.

Tabitha flung her hem back down to her knees. "Why did you keep looking?"

"You have cute underwear."

It was a lie, and Tabitha knew it. Her pale yellow panties weren't cute. He didn't fool her. It was her smooth, unblemished legs that enchanted him, and that realization actually made her feel better.

Logan cleared his throat and pulled away. Fortunately, he also knew this was no time to be distracted by such pleasant emotions. He snatched his shirt from her and hurriedly shrugged it on and buttoned himself up.

Tabitha returned her focus to matters of life and death. "Where's Rose? Why did you leave her?"

"To save you, fool!" he barked.

That left Tabitha feeling ungrateful. With her head down, she said, "Thank you, Logan."

His words were reassuring. "I left her with my mom. And before you say anything, Mom was coming back to reality. Also, the police were just getting to the church when I came after you."

"Do you have the slightest clue about what's happening?" Tabitha threw the question at Logan.

He shrugged. Both sat quietly for a few more moments.

Tabitha reflected on the events that had unfolded today, trying to put the incidents together to form an answer. Meanwhile, the tall pines swayed in the wind. A pinecone dropped and crunched under someone's foot.

Into the clearing stepped the form of a beautiful, dark-haired young woman.

Startled, Logan leaped to his feet and helped Tabitha up to greet the stranger. He became instantly entranced at the uncanny beauty of the young woman standing in front of him. Silky black hair lined her back, falling in perfectly straight lines to her waist, like a cape behind an hourglass figure accentuated by her tight clothes. Her eyes were dark brown, almost black, wicked even, like they belonged to an alien with an unknown agenda.

She greeted them. "Hello. Sorry to disturb you, but I'm staying in a cabin back here." She motioned behind her. "Are you Tabitha and Logan?"

Logan, already spellbound by the stranger's appearance, was speechless.

Tabitha spoke first. "Yeah, that's us."

"I'm Dusty." A friendly smile stretched her mouth into an exaggerated curve, but it could have been authentic. Tabitha couldn't determine either way, but something about Dusty spooked her. It wasn't just how she looked; it was an aura she gave off that chilled Tabitha.

Dusty shook off the smile and said, "I believe I have your sister, Rose, in my cabin, and, poor thing, she scraped her knee."

An alarm went off in Tabitha. Her sister could be in danger, and she couldn't trust the world today; something's afoot, and this Dusty was part of it.

"Where's your cabin? Is she OK? Let's go." Not giving Dusty any time to respond, Tabitha was already walking, with a limp, in the direction the stranger had pointed.

"Rose is OK," Dusty called after Tabitha, who was already several paces ahead. She turned her attention to Logan. "You must be Logan?"

"Yeah," he stammered.

Within a few steps, Tabitha saw the cabin and rushed to the door. She pushed it open, and dust billowed before her, dispersing through the single room. It seemed uninhabited. But inside the musty space, Rose sat on a tiny bed, light upon her from the cabin's only window. At first, Rose was frozen still, ghost-like, but the sight of her big sister animated her. She sprang up off the bed.

Tabitha sighed, "Hey there, little one. How did you get way out here?"

"I don't remember," Rose replied, hugging Tabitha's leg.

This time lapse bothered Tabitha; she looked back at Logan, hoping to flash him a warning with her eyes, so he could join on a quest to help. But he and Dusty were just entering the cabin, and while busily describing all his adventures, Logan didn't take his eyes off Dusty for one second, not even to greet Rose. Tabitha noticed something else: while Logan described the culmination of the natural or unnatural forces they had battled today, Dusty looked almost amused. Logan couldn't see this, Tabitha realized. *He's hooked!* He had bitten—hard—on the lure Dusty had dropped somewhere along the short walk to the cabin. He was being reeled in, *but for what purpose?*

As the only one self-aware, Tabitha concluded that she alone had to fight whatever danger lurked around her, hiding and waiting to spring an ambush. She swallowed that feeling and bent down to Rose. "Let me see that knee." Surveying that minor scrape, Tabitha kissed Rose on the forehead. "You'll be fine, little one."

But her sister wasn't fine. Rose appeared suspiciously groggy, like she was just waking from a nap. *She's been drugged.* With alarm bells going off in her head, Tabitha immediately examined Rose for any other signs of injury. Thankfully, none came to light.

She extended her examination to their new surroundings. The cabin creaked, maybe from the wind. Above the bed hung a wooden frame that held a stenciled sentence: *The quick brown fox jumps over the lazy dog.*

Tabitha had no idea what to make of that strange statement. As she tried to puzzle out what it meant, she felt Rose's finger spelling something on her leg. Tabitha looked down and Rose lowered her head and shook it, signaling *No, don't look at me.* Tabitha couldn't believe it; her five-year-old sister was trying to say something without Dusty or even the room itself knowing. Maybe Tabitha wasn't the only one self-aware after all. Tabitha stood up straight and pretended to study the framed sentence.

Tabitha had registered the first three letters of Rose's message, S, T, A, when Logan finally broke from Dusty and waved at Rose. "Hello, cutie! Are you OK?"

"I'm good," Rose said but continued spelling: Y, I, N.

Dusty rushed over to give Rose what was meant to seem like a playful poke in the stomach. In a manner that Tabitha instantly pegged as phony, she gushed, "She's a cutie, isn't she!" The spelling stopped when Dusty squatted beside Rose and grinned that ambiguous grin.

Tabitha was perplexed. What did Rose mean by spelling *Stay In?* Was she even done writing? Had Dusty scared her? And why didn't Rose remember ending up here? Then Tabitha caught something behind Dusty's smiling gaze that she hadn't caught outside: that broad smile half-hid an astuteness, along with a daring, threatening undertone that reminded Tabitha of a villain pretending to be good. Maybe the brown hues in the dimly lit cabin had brought out the darkness in Dusty's face. From deeper inside.

Dusty straightened up and addressed Tabitha. "You probably should get back to the church." Behind the fake affection, she sounded almost demanding. "Logan just told me about your day. And what a day! I'm sorry you had to witness all that you have, but I bet your parents just took shelter in the woods till the tornado passed. They're most likely at the church right now." Bending to look at Rose, she added, "Looking for you girls."

Tabitha sensed there was a catch to her words. Under the cadence of Dusty's voice was a push for them to head back to the church, not for their own safety but because the three of them were part of Dusty's plan in some way.

Tabitha couldn't bear to be around Dusty for one more second, so she pretended to oblige. "You're right. We should head back!"

She caught Logan's eye but he was pouting. He had fallen into a sulk, Tabitha could tell. He didn't want to leave Dusty's presence. Tabitha clenched Rose's hand and headed for the door, determined to leave with or without Logan.

"Be careful, guys," Dusty called behind them.

"We will." Tabitha nudged Logan. "Come on, Logan. I'm sure Miss Diana is wondering where you are." Already outside, Tabitha waited while Logan lingered in the cabin's doorway, taking a slow, reluctant step after her. *He has to be under a real-life spell,* Tabitha thought. After everything she'd seen today, spells weren't out of the realm of possibility.

Dusty and Logan said "Bye" to each other.

Dusty followed with, "Be sure you head back to the church and hug your mom."

Logan just nodded.

All three quietly walked away. Looking back one more time, Tabitha saw Dusty watching them from the doorway. *To make sure we obeyed and headed back.* Tabitha shouted, "This is the way back, right?"

"Yeah, you're going the right way," Dusty echoed from her cabin.

Tabitha knew they were heading toward the church, but felt an instinct to appease this woman who appeared out of nowhere. Who stayed in the middle of nowhere. And who had Logan fixated. Out of pure fear, Tabitha pretended to obey. Her gut told her the next time she saw Dusty, it wouldn't be playful smiles; it would be her full power on display.

Once the cabin was entirely out of sight, Tabitha stopped and questioned Rose. "Stay in? Stay in what?"

Logan looked confused.

Rose answered unequivocally, "Stay in the forest."

"Why, Rose?"

"Because a lady in my dream told me to stay in the forest and not go back."

Logan spoke up. "That's just a dream, Rose. We have to head ba—"

"No, we don't," Tabitha interjected. "Logan, listen to me. Something tells me that we need to stay here in the forest. That Rose's dream was a warning of some kind. It's not safe to head back. Not yet, anyway. You didn't see anything suspicious with Dusty?"

Fully charged now, Logan snapped back. "No! Are you crazy? It's not safe here in the forest! That wolf that dragged you is still out there, probably back among its pack. Plus, your leg needs attention! Look at it!"

Tabitha now feared Logan's aggression. She tried to defuse it, pleading with him, "Logan, please. This day has been off ever since we saw Saris's hand slide down that window. You have to admit: it's very strange for a woman to be staying alone in that little cabin out in the middle of nowhere. She made it a point to tell us to head back. I don't trust her. Something's afoot. There's a catch to us heading back."

Logan seemed open-minded and heartened by Tabitha's voice, but once her words stopped, he inhaled something that changed him. Something ancient that drifted on the wind.

It's the air as it existed here hundreds of years ago, Tabitha knew somehow.

That uncanny oxygen filled Logan's nostrils and sparked a masculinity that's present, even if dead or dying, in all men. He glared at Tabitha and insisted, "We are going back! If I have to drag you the whole way, like that wolf did!"

Rose clung tighter to her sister as Tabitha tried reasoning with him. "Logan, if you want to go back, you can. But leave us here. Why do we have to go with you?"

Logan's teeth clenched. "Because!" The modern teenager in him was long gone. Transformed into someone else—someone dangerous.

CHAPTER 23
Lily

I squeezed Lily, took her all in, but something was missing. The warmth, her fragrance. *Her.* I unlocked my mama-bear hold and allowed Tyler space to hug as I came to grips—that Lily was a ghost with a touchable shell, but still a ghost.

She spoke. "Mom, it's me." I could hear it now. It was her, the soul of my daughter.

All the words I wanted to say flooded me at once. "Lily, I love you! I'm so sorry I couldn't protect you as your mother. I failed, and you paid the price. You deserved better."

Lily stepped from her dad's burrow, touched my arm, and folded herself around me. And in her enclave, I could feel nothing but forgiveness and unwavering love. She wore a bright yellow dress that I recognized as the one my grandma had sewn by hand for Lily's thirteenth birthday. All my emotions condensed into one—satisfaction. A wind gusted from the field, interrupting and reminding me that we had a world to save. Lily let go, and something zapped from my body, the something that had briefly stopped the trains and relieved the pressing weight. However, the satisfaction of seeing her again still simmered underneath, making everything bearable enough for me to soldier on.

Her eyes carried a worldly wisdom now as she spoke to Tyler and me, in words that showed a wisdom far beyond her years. "I only have a few minutes before I disappear into my role. So let me explain quickly: As you know, Mom—and you're starting to learn, Dad—Mother Nature is divided into forces of good and evil. These forces can lodge themselves into your mind. What Mist hasn't explained fully to you yet: there's a level of free will inside you that can't be broken. In order to fight that and strengthen your free will, you need to access and use the logical part of your mind. Evil is actually not logical. That's because humans are adept enough to come up with solutions without sacrificing someone else. Solving their problems at someone else's expense. Essentially, evil is unnecessary. Remember: if either of your lives is at stake, always hang on to logic."

Lily turned her full attention to Tyler and continued, "Dad, if Mom gets hurt so bad she needs to go to the hospital, you can't take her. Not unless you want to kill almost four billion people. This virus is highly contagious and deadly. Right now, some of these eleven parents out here will fight you, and I can only help you in subtle ways."

Lily paused and I could already see the "good bye" in her eyes. "This is the last time you can see me this way. Still, before you get sad—" she now looked directly at me.

I struggled to suppress the sweet sorrow from spilling down my cheeks.

"I'm always around," she said, "even if you can't see me, and if you want to talk to me, you can. Even if I can't respond, know that I'm listening."

The three of us hugged one last time, Tyler and I clung all the more tightly to our daughter, not wanting to let go.

Lily whispered, "Now go save the world before the force field around the parents gives way. I love you, Mom and Dad."

I realized I had closed my eyes to blink away my tears, because when I opened them, she was gone. Tyler and I held our arms out, suspended around empty air. We dropped our hands. The touchable shell of Lily had vanished, but this left me hopeful, not sad, because, as she said, "I'm always around."

I waved at Tyler, knocking loose his gaze through the air Lily had just occupied, long enough to tell us everything.

It was time to enlist Tyler in this war. "You ready to spend a month in the forest with eleven worried parents?"

"Yeah, we got this." He looked confidently at me. "It's going to be tough, but we got this." I knew he was including Lily in *We got this.* Homey, familial warmth coursed through me, easing the duress I'd been under ever since David had tried to kill me yesterday.

I felt myself swelling with the same confidence and repeated, "We got this."

Tyler and I were heading toward the woods when a girl's scream stopped us.

"Help!!! Ah, no, help! No—"

The scream came from the field. And in the middle, I saw the grass dropping, like a row of dominoes, in a path that led to the forest.

I couldn't see the girl, but I figured she was being dragged through the grass. I started to run out to help, but Tyler seized my arm. A young man ran after the girl as I fought with Tyler.

"What are you doing? That girl is being dragged! It must be the same wolf that attacked us earlier!"

"*Logan, help!*" the girl screamed.

"Don't you see, Misty? That girl has been infected! Lily's making that wolf drag her away."

"Oh, my goodness. You don't think Lily would kill that poor girl? And the boy that's chasing after her?"

"If she feels it's necessary to save the world, yes. They will be killed." It sounded cold how Tyler said it, but I knew what he meant; maybe the only logical course of action was to kill them.

With that thought, I abandoned my battle to save them. The girl and boy disappeared into the woods ahead of us, their fate unknown to me. That left me with a sadness I had to push away—and push away quickly—because I saw the first police making their way around to the back of the church.

We couldn't get caught up in that investigation. Tyler and I disappeared ourselves among the trees that would be our shields for the next thirty days. We hurried, at a near run, and while we did, I wondered how Lily would keep the police from searching the woods and finding us. Counting the parents, the boy and girl, Tyler and me, fifteen people would be reported as missing. No doubt a thorough search would follow. Was it up to Tyler and me to avoid the police? As I questioned our duty, I began to hear agitated shouting. It was the eleven parents. Their cries led us to a round opening that had been carved in the forest, holding them all.

Some were trying to run the circle's edge but were knocked back by the invisible force field. Their shouts showed how angry that cage was making them. I would be angry, too. I understood the parents' frustration, but knew we had to make them listen to us. The world was at stake. Tyler pulled out Saris's gun. I'd forgotten he still had that. Seeing him shirtless made me wish he had his police uniform on. That would have helped show the extra authority and trust we needed. That made me take a critical look at myself. Tyler's buttoned-up dress shirt was hanging on me, barely covering my ass, with no pants on. I wasn't dressed for the occasion either, but luckily I still had my bra and panties on; this white shirt wouldn't fully conceal my body.

Seeing us coming out from under the trees, the parents shifted their anger in our direction. They shouted over each other.

"What is really going on?"

"Who are you?"

"Why are we in here?"

"Where is my daughter?"

"Where is my son?"

I stopped at what I guessed was the force field line and tried to explain. "Let me start from the beginning. Our daughter died three years ago . . ." I summarized the distant past and then got to the present with more detail, starting with David, the intruder who had tried to kill me yesterday. Surprisingly, the parents stayed quiet as I recounted each increasingly unbelievable event that had led up to today and this moment. I even told them about my affair with Saris and that he was the one who had hired David to kill my daughter. Especially when I got into the Mother Nature part, I expected shouts of disbelief. Hoping to win their trust, I was surprised to see that Tyler was holding the gun out. I wished he would put it away as a sign of good faith. But none of the parents said anything. I finished with, "So we have to stay in these woods for thirty days, for your kids, and for the safety of the whole world."

A woman began to cry. She moaned, "You're saying . . . half of us will die?"

A man shouted, "Fuck this! You shot my wife!" It was Becky's husband. He glared at Tyler, pushed through the other parents and walked straight toward Tyler.

I gulped. Sometime during my story, the force field had dropped.

Without warning, Tyler shot the man. His blood spattered from a hole in his leg, and he collapsed.

I screamed, "Tyler! He has a kid!! You could have at least given him a warning!"

While chastising Tyler, I could see someone else move in the circle. I shouted, "Stop! Or he's gonna shoot you, too!"

The woman complied, fear splashed across her face.

Tyler threatened the whole group. "Anyone else move, I will shoot you in the head and not the leg! Now someone help this man."

The man he shot—Becky's husband—wailed on the ground, clutching his wound. The red-haired guy ran over and attended to him.

While that went on, I further explained, "There's an old house somewhere in here, and we need to go there. It will give us the shelter we'll need."

All the parents seemed to be on the same page now, but I knew Tyler and I had to be watchful for anyone straying away. I wasn't sure how many bullets that gun had left. It was Saris's gun, after all.

Once Becky's husband leg was wrapped up, Tyler ordered, "OK, everyone, let's go." On the far side of the circle we saw a clear path, so we guessed that was the way to the house. Then the woods rustled. Wind swirled up from the soil and blew only in front of us. It raised woodland debris in a pair of howling walls, an unspoken order to change direction.

Tyler and I looked at each other and, in unison, said, "Lily."

She was guiding us.

"This way," Tyler commanded. "Everyone this way."

The parents pivoted and trudged along. I could almost feel the cloud of sadness hanging above them. They didn't seem fazed in the least by this unnatural phenomenon. I assumed they were all thinking about everything I had unloaded on them: they're infected with a virus, they won't see their kids for a month, half will die, and we're at war with nature.

Tyler took the lead; I followed behind everyone. Pinecones, small branches, dirt, and leaves all swirled in the air on either side of us, but not overhead, creating a roofless tunnel. Up ahead, I couldn't see an end to it yet, but figured it would end. I wanted to reach out and touch this wind-driven wall but feared my fingers would be sliced. This phenomenon, maybe something like the force field that had confined them before, could help the parents understand that we were battling nature on a scale we'd never seen before. After all, they had seen the bats, the tornado, the force field circle, and now this wind tunnel.

The seconds became minutes and then hours. The wind continued its never-ending guide, singularly focused, leaving the rest of the woods still. Our steps became labored with the high sun beaming on us through the trees, indicating it was around noon. The day warmed to a muggy heat. Thankfully, it wasn't sweltering, but everyone grew increasingly frustrated by the distance we had walked, with no end in sight. The discomfort from the wounds in my legs rose with each step, but I pushed the feeling back, focused on studying the parents.

I could sense resistance brewing silently among them. Just when I thought everyone would bolt off in a "fuck-this" move, the tunneling wind before us stopped. Through the silent trees, we saw a two-story plantation-style house surrounded by a canopy of tall pines. It must have been white once, but was now faded to gray. It might have laid dormant for two hundred years. Once majestic, it had weathered into something a teenager would have made a game of dare, a test of courage.

Subdued whispers were the only sound.

Tyler broke the semi-silence. "Everyone get on the porch."

The parents hobbled onto the veranda that wrapped around the front and one side of the house.

I was the last one to step onto the brick steps when I heard a voice behind me. The hair on my neck raised with fright, and I spun around to face a young man. He looked like the teenage boy who had chased after the screaming girl in the field.

He babbled, "I had to do it. I had to do it. I had to do it." He didn't have his shirt on, and his body was dirty like he'd been rolling—maybe fighting?—on the ground. Then I noticed something even more alarming: his hands were covered in blood, and some was splattered on his chest.

One of the fathers recognized him and asked, "Logan, have you seen our daughters? Tabitha and Rose?"

Immediately, I saw regret in this boy's eyes. I dreaded what I knew he was about to admit.

Remorsefully, Logan answered, "I killed Tabitha."

CHAPTER 24

Thirty Minutes Ago

Tabitha knew her life, and Rose's, too, were in grave danger if they didn't comply with Logan. So she agreed, "OK, Logan, you win. We'll head back to the church."

He cocked his head in the direction he wanted them to go, following the disturbed soil where the red wolf had dragged Tabitha. It was the obvious pathway back to the church.

Tabitha obeyed and quietly began to walk with Rose in tow. She kept a close watch on Logan, who was breathing in and out like a beast readying itself to pounce on its prey. She didn't want to say another word; the air between her and Logan felt like a tinderbox. Any sudden movements or disobedient sounds from her would strike a match, igniting the violence simmering inside him.

As the seconds passed, she continued to ponder what was possessing Logan. Had Dusty done this to him? Why was he so insistent on heading back—forcing them along? Could she somehow siphon out the demon that had lodged itself in him? Would she have to perform an exorcism of some sort? Where had that cute dimpled guy with the infectious smile gone? He had been with her less than thirty minutes ago. She wanted him back. Needed him back. The farther down the path Tabitha walked, the more loudly her gut instinct began to sound off, warning, *Don't go back to church.* But that meant she would have to fight Logan; the demon inside him was determined to forge ahead.

Tabitha tried to ignore that instinct, but it kept pressing her, along with the thought that her parents were there in the woods somewhere. *You can't leave them.* And with that thought, she decided to halt Logan's march to the church. She whispered, "Rose, run to that tree and wait for me."

Rose darted off, not wasting any time.

Tabitha knew Rose remembered the dream that had warned her to stay in the woods. She knew Rose had complete confidence and trust in her older sister.

Tabitha turned quickly to confront Logan, now visibly angry at Rose's disobedience. She cajoled him, "Wait. Logan. Please."

He stalked toward her, vile contempt frozen upon his face, with no sign of defrosting.

"Logan, I just want to find my mom and dad. Please don't hur—"

He shoved her down.

The air was knocked out of her before she could finish the plea. Before her breath came back, he had already seized her hand. Logan dragged Tabitha violently down the same path the wolf had made.

Like a barking chihuahua, Rose sprang out from behind a tree and yelled, "Leave my sister alone! Let her go! Logan, let her go!"

Seizing a chance to free herself, Tabitha spun about and fought through the pine straw and dirt until, suddenly, her head struck a tree trunk.

Logan could feel the fighting weight in his hand change into dead weight. He stopped. His chest still heaved demonically. But as he exhaled, the evil slowly seeped out.

Rose cried out, "Tabby, Tabby!" She tugged at an unresponsive Tabitha but couldn't wake her. Rose started weeping and curled herself beside her big sister.

Logan focused his mind to brush away the remaining demonic possession, and awoke to the reality of what he'd done.

He dropped Tabitha's lifeless hand. Instantly, crushing guilt washed over him. Logan turned to see what he hoped was just a dream: Tabitha lying motionless, with a trickle of blood coming from her hairline. He crouched to get a closer look, and Rose threw a fit. "No! No! Leave us alone!" she bawled. "You hurted her!"

"I'm—" Logan stopped, speechless. He didn't know what to say, had no idea how to ease Rose's trauma. Then he heard a snort and immediately saw the wolf. Its drooling mouth, sharp teeth bared, grinned inches from Tabitha's head. The animal must have crept up after smelling her blood.

Logan shot up and hurled his weight onto the wolf. It fought back viciously, but inflamed anger sent adrenaline through Logan's muscles as he held his own. This anger was stronger than the demonic fury he'd acted out just minutes before. The battle between animal and man drew on for long minutes as they wrestled on the forest floor. Logan got his arm wrapped in a death grip around the beast, narrowly avoiding its chomping canines at every turn.

Eventually, Logan managed to get the right grip under the wolf's jaw and, with all his strength, yanked its head up and back. A sickening crack told him he'd broken its neck. The struggling beast stopped struggling. Blood surged from the animal's jaws and covered his hands. Logan unlatched his hands of death. Just like Tabitha, the wolf lay motionless on the soil.

Logan sat on his knees and roared out the bittersweet victory, "Aaaahhhhwwwwww!"

He hadn't wanted to kill the wolf but felt he had no choice. Logan looked around for where he had left Tabitha and Rose but realized the battle had carried him deeper into the woods. With its blood dripping from his hands, he ran about, looking for his way back to Tabitha. He wanted to save her, if that was still possible. That "if" plagued his mind, along with *What in the hell came over me to treat Tabitha that way?* And he wondered: Would that violent impulse come back? He hated the lack of control he felt but vowed that he would try and fight off the possession next time.

His blue dress shirt hung in shreds. Some of the shirt stuck to him, with strips of fabric hanging loose and tickling him. He stripped it all off, getting some of the wolf's blood on his chest, and carried on shirtless.

Crunching his feet through the forest, he knew Tabitha was right about something important: heading back to the church is a mistake. But he didn't know why. Then, as he wandered, he saw an abandoned house in the distance. And people walking toward it.

CHAPTER 25

Day One

I watched the missing girl's father lunge toward the boy he called Logan, murderous vengeance on his face. Tyler and one other man stopped him from leaping off that porch and getting to him. The boy stood there sweating, his remorse obvious. I could tell he would have surrendered and allowed the father to beat him to death, or close to it. I suspected Dust had gotten into this boy's mind and used him to kill this man's daughter.

I yelled to get everyone's attention, but mainly this father and his equally distressed mother. Wailing, she was leaning against a wall. I recognized her as the woman with the sea-colored eyes I'd been so suspicious of back in the church corridor.

"Listen, everyone," I said. "He didn't have control of his mind. Dust got into his mind."

The boy swiveled his head toward me, his mouth hanging open. "Dusty! We met a woman named Dusty. Is that who you're talking about?" He pointed into the woods behind him. "She's staying in a cabin, somewhere in here. She looks different from any woman

I've ever seen. Could she have put a spell on me or something? I felt something taking over what I thought. What I did. Like a demon!" He gave me a pleading look, like he hoped I could help him to forgive himself. "I didn't have control."

Before I could explain to him that he had guessed correctly, the sobbing mother asked, "What about Rose? Did you see her?"

"Yeah, I did actually. She's alive." Logan's eyes dipped toward the ground. He couldn't look at her. "Rose is with Tabitha."

The mother leaped down the steps toward the boy and demanded, "Take me to her! Now!"

I reached out to keep the mother from getting closer to Logan. I could see the same sorrow and fury that had filled me after Lily died. I didn't have the heart to stop this woman from going out to find her surviving daughter. I turned to Tyler, then back to the mother, and said, "I'll go with you. We'll find her."

Tyler shook his head.

I nodded back to let him know that I was going no matter what. I felt for this mother. She had already lost a daughter. I couldn't have her lose another. Besides, if we ordered those two parents back inside that house, without making any effort to find their daughter, we wouldn't have any control over them.

The father declared, "I'm going with her."

Tyler replied right away, "No! You stay here!" He held the gun on him as a firm threat.

The mother tried to defuse the stand-off. "No, Daniel, you stay here. I'll bring the girls back."

I noticed the plural "girls" in her statement. *Is she expecting us to carry—*

She answered my question. "Logan will carry Tabitha back. That's the least he can do."

The dad yelled, "I don't want that boy touching my daughter!"

His wife pointed to me. "I believe this lady, and I believe Logan was possessed by something. Daniel, you can't deny how strange this has all been. Just think about how we got here."

The father appeared to understand enough to simmer down. She tearfully kissed her husband good bye.

I was relieved that she enlisted Logan to come with us; we need him as a guide.

When Tyler approached me, I expected a scolding, so I was surprised when he hugged me—while keeping a watchful eye on all the parents. The last thing we needed would be for any of them to dart off. He whispered, "I understand why you have to go. Both reasons: to prevent a revolt, and for your own tender heart. I love you, Misty." He kissed my forehead.

"I love you too, Tyler. What a weekend? Huh?"

"It's not over yet," he reminded me, and added a warning. "If Logan looks like he's being possessed again, stay away from him. He's just a teenager, but he looks strong."

"Don't worry; I have an angry mother on my side."

"Still, be careful. I wouldn't trust her, either."

"I will. I'm stronger than you realize."

"Oh, you have definitely proven that to me," he said, finally allowing himself a smile. But that must have reminded him about how I'd been hurt. "How are your legs? Are they hurting? I noticed a little limp on our way here."

"Tyler!" It was my warning not to probe my decision any further. *I'm going no matter what,* I resolved.

He backed off and gave me a quick kiss on the lips. "Love you, babe. See you back here soon."

"Love you."

He resumed his place on the porch.

I already missed his presence. The mother was waiting at my side, Logan on my other. With another look at the blood on his chest, I called to the parents on the porch, "Can I have someone's jacket?"

The men all wore their church suits except for the red-haired guy who'd given his up for Becky's husband. I realized that eight men, counting Tyler, stood on that porch with just three women. That made sense: two men had already lost their wives; and two more of us were down here. I assumed the red-haired guy was a single dad.

In a surprising move, Daniel—Tabitha's father—handed over his Sunday jacket for Logan to cover himself.

I passed it to Logan, who took it, pointed to the blood on his chest and told Daniel, "That's not Tabitha's blood. It's a wolf's. It wanted to eat Tabitha, and I killed it. With my hands."

Everyone stood silent at this. Then the mother asked, "What happened to her, then?"

Logan rocked himself, clearly dreading what he knew he had to say. "I dragged her on the ground," he said, with a sob, "until she hit her head on a tree. Then I noticed the wolf was at her head, about to grab her with its teeth. That's when . . . when I went after the wolf. I left Rose beside her."

The mother lit up. "Wait. That means you don't know for sure that you killed her?"

Logan shook his head. "She hit her head really hard, and she was bleeding."

The mother ran her hands through her hair. "We have to go now. We have to find her quickly. There's a chance she's alive, but she'll need help. I've got to find my baby."

Hurrying off into the forest, I could hear Daniel yell after us, "Bring our daughters home."

As we walked, I asked the mother, "What's your name?"

"Kelly."

"Sorry that we have to meet in these circumstances."

"I just want to find Rose and Tabitha." She sobbed, a dam of emotions almost breaking when she said Tabitha's name.

I tried to comfort her. "We will find them." That's all I felt I could say without setting her off into hysterics. I let her be, and turned my attention to Logan. "Do you know where we're going?"

"I don't. I've been lost. I was looking for Tabitha and Rose when I saw you guys."

"Wait." Something suddenly occurred to me. "A wolf dragged Tabitha from the churchyard, didn't it? And you were chasing after them? Weren't you?"

"How do you know that?"

"Because Tyler and I saw you."

That drew a sharp glare from Kelly. I was sure she was now blaming me for failing to save her daughter.

I didn't address her directly, but told Logan, "I couldn't chase after you guys because the force field was about to give way. Once it did, I knew all the parents would head back into the world and infect everybody." With that last part, I turned to face Kelly.

Her anger toward me appeared to

besides, she was focused on the hunt for her daug

woods for the slightest clue. I understood if this woma

contempt for me. I'd had a chance to save Tabitha but had

getting back to the parents a higher priority.

Timidly, Logan spoke up. "Force field? Infect everybody?"

"It's a long story. I'll tell you after we find the girls." I didn't feel like retelling the whole story of Mother Nature's wrath, Dust versus Mist, how this is their territory and they can manipulate us, and so forth. I had just gone over all that with the parents.

Logan didn't seemed too bothered that I didn't answer him. I could see he was inundated by regret. He would have to live with the knowledge he had killed someone.

The next few minutes drifted in a pattern: We would walk a bit, stop to look around, and yell, "Tabitha! Rose!" The forest echoed our calls; no one answered. Logan kept silent. I assumed he didn't want to scare the girls away. I realized I was feeling more sympathy for Logan than for Kelly. That felt strange; I could certainly relate to losing a daughter. But I had also experienced crushing guilt: the kind I had no doubt Logan was reeling from. That guilt had eaten at me when Lily died, and then again after I'd hired David to kill Tyler. I was so glad I had backed out of that arrangement. I couldn't imagine how guilty I would feel if I'd actually had Tyler killed. *Damn that Dust. She's too powerful.*

With that thought, I moved closer to Logan and said, "Dusty hijacked my mind, too. She tried to get me to kill my husband."

"But you didn't kill him," he protested. He had to let me know his story had ended far worse than mine.

ıg this wasn't over yet. "Yes,

ı a secret. You can fight Dusty,

ext time. I have a feeling you're

ι, too."

man and a boy. His creamy brown

ιe of hardship even before today—but

, help guide this boy; he needed a mother right now. He _ ι to know what was going on and what we were dealing with. As ve continued our search, I began to tell him the story, about everything that had led to now.

"And that's how you exercise your free will—think logically." I said, wrapping up my story and giving Logan a smile to reassure him that I had faith in him. "I don't think Dust will enter your mind again."

I could tell he felt better, less guilty. He held a faint smile for a moment as he said, "Thanks. Tabitha and I were both wondering what was up today."

As I retold my complicated story, I lost track of Kelly. I realized, with a jolt, that I didn't see her. Or hear her. Logan and I surveyed our surroundings. Everything was too silent. *Damn, damn, damn,* I thought. *Something's got her.*

"Where did she go?" Just as I asked, I heard a click.

"I don—" Logan gasped.

Oh, no. The gunshot echoed through the forest.

Logan clutched his stomach as he dropped, knees first. I was reaching out to help when I heard a woman's voice.

"Stop. Don't help him. He'll only be in the way," Kelly waved a gun at me.

Fuck it, I told myself. *This woman is tiny; I can take her.* I just had to dodge her bullets. In full rage, I bolted at her, and she shot at me. The bullet grazed my hip; I rammed her into the ground and twisted the pistol from her hand. I slapped her face with the gun's handle; blood shot out of her nose. That angered me more: *I've seen enough fucking blood this weekend.* I had known I couldn't trust her. I should have trusted my instincts.

I sat on Kelly, locking her to the ground. I had her where I wanted her. *I'm going to kill this woman.* "Let me guess. You've been working for Saris."

"Yelllp," she strained to say.

"The only thing is," I wondered aloud, "why didn't you just go back to the church yourself? If you're infected, you can go back and infect the world. You didn't have to shoot Logan."

"No," she gasped. "We are Dust's helpers, and she made us immune. We can't be infected. I needed somebody who could be infected; I was going to use that gun to force you back. Or even take my girls with me. Since I can't find my them, I chose you. Too much trouble to keep the gun on both of you. So I shot Logan."

"Are you Saris's last helper?" I asked. I didn't trust her to tell me the truth.

"Maybe. Maybe not."

Of course, I'd expected a snide answer.

Behind me, Logan moaned in anguish. I had to help him, but couldn't release Kelly. That meant I had to kill her. I pointed the gun at her skull.

Seeing her fate, she launched into a confession. "Tell my daughters I did it for humanity's future. You told Logan that Dust brainwashes you. Well, I wasn't brainwashed. This planet is over-populated. Think of what it will mean not to have so many people? Maybe you know that the black plague wiped out forty percent of the world's population in the 1300s. And after that the world entered a renaissance."

Before she could continue her twisted history lesson, I closed my eyes and shot her point-blank. Her body shuddered under my knees and then went still.

I inspected the bullet hole in her forehead to make sure I'd killed her before jumping up to attend to Logan. Despite pressing his hands against his abdomen, the wound bled profusely. I felt optimistic about his survival because the bullet seemed to have penetrated his side, likely missing any vital organ. I stripped Daniel's church jacket off him and wrapped it around his blood-soaked belly. As I worked, I remembered doing almost exactly the same thing to Tyler's wolf bite this morning.

"Listen: we have to get you back to that house. We can get back to searching for Tabitha and Rose later."

He squeezed out the words, "No. We have to find Tabitha and Rose. Stop them . . ." he moaned from the pain. "They're infected."

"What do you mean? How are they infected? Did those bats get into the classroom?" With a cold chill in my gut, I remembered Kelly just saying that she intended to force her daughters back. *So they are infected.*

Logan answered, "Tabitha went out the back of the church to look for her parents."

Seeing the girl's dead mother lying behind me wasn't setting well in my stomach, but I had to hear him out.

"And when she was outside," Logan went on, "a bat swooped down and bit her."

I pieced together my own recollections and said, "That's when the wolf dragged her. But wait: was the wolf helping her?"

"I thought that, too. She also had a snake bite below where the wolf bit her. I thought the wolf's bite was a good thing, by letting her bleed. It was drawing the venom out of her leg. Now I realize it was doing something else important. Not just pulling out the venom, but also pulling her away from people."

"Does a part of you believe Tabitha's alive?" I asked.

"I have my doubts, but Rose is alive for sure. But by now, if she's near Tabitha, she's already been infected, too."

"OK," I said. "Before we head back to the house, we'll look for them."

The improvised bandage had suppressed the blood flow from his bullet wound. I lifted him, and though he grunted through the hurt, he seemed OK. Now, he was fixated on trudging ahead. We both walked a few steps when he said, "Wait, you're wounded."

Mentally, I did an *Oh yeah, my-hip*. Seeing some red, I lifted Tyler's oversize shirt and peeled back my panties. It didn't look like more than a scrape. The blood had already dried around it. After everything else I'd been through, this didn't worry me. Kelly's bullet had literally just grazed me. "I'll be fine."

Logan and I forged ahead. Until I heard a trickling stream, I didn't realize how thirsty I was. We stopped for a much-needed drink of water, which revitalized me for another mile or so. Now I started to worry about Tyler, back with the parents. I had to wonder if someone else was still working for Saris, for Dust. Was there someone like Kelly in our midst? At that moment, I felt my daughter's presence.

Lily's words whispered through my head, *No, Mom, that's the last follower of Saris. But Dust can bring evil out of almost anyone, like she did Logan. So be careful.*

I stopped suddenly, startling Logan. I wanted to ask Lily something else, but her warm presence was already gone. I had to explain to a curious Logan, "My daughter just talked to me. Kelly was the last one working for Saris, but we still have to watch the others carefully."

Telling Logan that made me realize that I trusted him. He could be an ally of Tyler and me.

The shadows under the trees around us had grown longer and deeper. Most of the afternoon must have passed; the sun was just an hour or so away from setting. My legs hummed with only a slight pain, which made me thankful. I had grown weary about finding Tabitha and Rose, and I could see the same resignation in Logan. But I knew—and he agreed—we had to soldier on even if it got dark. We couldn't risk the girls going back to the church or stumbling into the world some other way. I had to do everything I could. Four billion lives depended on it.

Then a thought haunted me. Wouldn't it be easier just to kill all the parents? Everyone exposed to the virus? *Eliminate all risks.* I shook off the thought. *Nice try, Dust.* I remembered Lily's words: *there's a level of free will inside you that can't be broken. In order to fight that and strengthen your free will, you need to access and use the logical part of your mind. Evil is actually not logical. That's because*

*humans are adept enough to come up with solutions without sacri-
ficing someone else. Solving their problems at someone else's expense.
Essentially, evil is unnecessary.*

CHAPTER 26

Sunday Dusk

Tabitha awoke with a splitting headache that stripped her mind of clear thought. Her eyes creaked open to the reddish colors of dusk strung across the sky. Hours had gone by, she worried. But to her relief, she found Rose curled up next to her, asleep. She wet her lips and tasted dried blood. Then she heard footsteps in the distance. Her body ached as she strained to sit up and see who it was. Then she saw him. *Logan.*

She dropped, pressing herself against the ground again. The sudden motion woke Rose.

Tabitha whispered, "Shh. Stay down."

Rose obeyed without question, her eyes reflecting her joy that her big sister was alive.

Even through her foggy awakening, Tabitha remembered that Logan had almost killed her. Now, she feared, he was searching for her to finish the job. *How did Logan lose track of me?* Tabitha wondered, *He was dragging me.* Then, echoing over the distant footsteps, she heard a voice.

"Tabitha! Rose! Are you there?" It wasn't Logan, but instead, a woman's voice. It sounded trustworthy. But how many others had she trusted today who had turned against her? Tabitha didn't know what to do. Should she reveal herself to this woman? Who was this person, and why was she with Logan? *Is it Dusty?* It didn't sound like Dusty, but that sinister presence in this forest was definitely deceitful enough to disguise her voice and lure them out.

Tabitha decided to stay put, hoping to remain unseen as the two walked by. She couldn't risk an encounter, especially not with Logan. She had to protect Rose in the only way she knew how. Tabitha assumed the defensive stance: trust no one.

Logan and the woman eventually moved on. The only signs of life came from the trees as their branches brushed among themselves with the occasional wind. Tabitha shivered, not from a wind chill, but at the realization that she couldn't leave these woods.

Stay in the forest became an emblazoned motto that advised her intuition. Whatever had possessed Logan wasn't of Good Nature. That much she had clearly deciphered hours before when her eyes had locked onto his. That had told her Logan was some kind of pawn, directed by evil tentacles that stretched through these woods, trying to yank her back to civilization. On an invisible level, she had also detected the arms of good that, for now at least, were embracing her. She fretted about how tenuous that hold was, especially after dark fell. The inevitability of night haunted her for another reason. She could foresee both of them lying in the darkness, prey for creatures that hunt at night. She felt doubly alone because Rose was only five; she couldn't share what it really meant to stay in these woods at night.

One thing she was sure of: they shouldn't remain here. Painfully, Tabitha got up and started walking, Rose following close alongside. She muddled through the agony, in her head and virtually everywhere else. Steadfastly, she pressed forward, scouting her surroundings for somewhere they could hole up before night fell. All the while, she clung to fading hope that she'd discover both parents alive and well. The defiant teenager that she'd been lately had shrunk away, diminishing her independence to longing for what she'd needed when she was younger, her father's hug and consoling words, "Everything will be all right."

Another five minutes and the horizon was swallowing the sun. Tabitha and Rose's pathless trek had led to nowhere because Tabitha didn't yet know what somewhere looked like. She was lost and wanted to be found by someone who loved her. With each passing second, loneliness crept further in, darkening her spirit. Then, in the still forest, she heard moaning. It awakened her. A mental light broke through, pulling her back from a precipice that dropped into an endless black abyss. Dimly visible beyond the trunks of eight or nine big pine trees someone was lying down. In the dim twilight, she registered the blue patterned dress on this person as her mama's. "Mom? Is that you?"

"Tabby, Rose," came the faint answer. "Are you there?"

A flush of energy washed over Tabitha as she raced toward her mama. Rose, squealing with delight, followed.

"Mom, we're here," Tabitha said, a mere second before she saw her mama's face.

The grotesque sight was like a sucker punch to her heart, bringing forth hot tears. With the amount of blood everywhere, she wondered, *How is she alive?* Still, she was thankful.

Kelly whispered, "Girls, I love you both dearly."

Rose placed her little hand on her mama's arm and rubbed, her gesture of reassurance, displaying both maturity and composure in the face of her mother's dire injury.

Tabitha fought through the tears to say, "Mom, I love you so much. Please stay with us."

Kelly choked back the blood coming from her mouth and said, "Girls, I don't have much time on this earth. Your dad is waiting for you back at the church. You need to get out of these woods. It's not safe."

Tabitha's heart sank. *Oh, no.* Mom was one of the evil tentacles, trying to persuade her to go back to civilization. Her tears slowed, and she reasoned, *Mom is a vessel. Like Logan was.* Something or someone evil was using her to do their bidding. *Dusty?* The sadness, still palpable, was overwhelming because, possessed or not, her mom was about to die.

Tabitha knowingly lied to her dying mother, "Yes, Mom, we'll head back. I love you. I love you."

Rose hollered, "Mommy! Mommy, don't die. Don't go!"

Kelly spoke struggling to draw breath, drowning in her own blood, "Rose, I have to. But I'll always be with you. I love you both very much. I did it all for you two. Goodbye, girls—" Her voice bubbled the final words. Kelly's eyes closed, and her body stopped moving. She died precisely as the sun's last ray vanished from the western sky.

Tabitha cupped both hands on her face and cried. Beside her, Rose did the same. Further minutes drifted by and, eventually, both girls broke their crying spell. They hugged each other to push back the anguish. After all, not only was their mother gone, they were still alone in the dark woods.

Tabitha imagined a predator's eyes cast hungrily upon them, shining through the black night. The chilling thought sent a shiver that knocked the image from her thoughts. She refocused on getting up and moving, to keep that image far, far away.

Much as she hated to leave her mom lying there, she felt they had to get moving, sensing that answers awaited her somewhere beyond here. Tabitha and Rose kissed their mother one last time and then turned away. The light from the rising moon was their savior, casting enough light to guide them. Otherwise, the girls would have been in total darkness.

After only a minute of walking, Tabitha was struck with thirst and hunger pains, but mostly thirst. She knew Rose had to be suffering the same thing. Hoping to find water, she was relieved to stumble upon a small pond. Its dark, unmoving surface looked creepy in the dark. Tabitha approached the water's edge and wondered what else was thirsty tonight. Not wanting to linger, she quickly cupped the water into her mouth.

Rose, watching her sister, started to do the same, but Tabitha stopped her.

You can't see what's underneath, she reminded herself. Tabitha cupped the water. "OK, Rose, I got you. Now open wide." She tipped her hand to let Rose get a drink. Some spilled, but Tabitha did this three more times until Rose had enough. Tabitha was reaching for another drink for herself when she saw movement in water. Breaking the pond's surface were the red eyes of an alligator. And then another pair of eyes, and then another. Three gators were heading towards them.

Tabitha leaped up, seized Rose's hand, and fled. Rose hadn't noticed what Tabitha saw. Tabitha pulled Rose through the dark forest so fast her little feet could barely keep pace, almost tripping several times, yanked back up by her persistent sister. Then Tabitha stopped.

A man-shaped shadow caught her eyes. He was standing about ten feet to their left. She had almost run past him. Was this a friend or a foe? It wasn't Logan; this unknown man was bulkier. Tabitha questioned herself. *Should I keep running? Should I? Should I?*

Instead, she boldly asked, "Who are you?"

CHAPTER 27
The Beginning of the End

Night was getting closer and closer, and I was getting badly worried. Were we ever going to find those girls?

Logan stopped. Sounding forlorn, he said, "We need to go back to that house."

"No, we need to find them," I insisted, and kept walking.

"Rose or Tabitha—if she's alive—neither one of them is going to leave these woods," he declared.

"How can you be so sure?" I halted and listened for his response.

"That's why I dragged Tabitha. Because she refused to head back to the church. And Rose was the one that told her it wasn't a good idea. Now that I think about it, I'll bet your daughter Lily was somehow influencing them to stay."

I believed him, but I wasn't sure if letting those two girls—or that one little girl—stay overnight in these woods was a good idea. Also, I had no clue how to get back to the house. We had walked miles upon miles, in many different directions. I studied the landscape around me. Logan and I had found ourselves in more of a savanna than a forest: the longleaf pines were spaced well apart, jutting above a plain of tall grass and short, bright-green shrubs that extended as far as the eye could see. Their grayish trunks looked dead until you looked at their forest-green tops, swaying with life, soaking up the last morsel of sunlight. The sun was perched directly on the horizon, unobstructed by the usual dense woodlands. A white haze slightly dimmed its brightness, but its center held a bright yellow hue, reminding me of a cracked-open egg. This area had a sweet smell, like green plants after a spring rain. It was all tranquil and soothing, like everything had been put on pause. The survival trains that had roared through me all weekend had come to a halt. Logan also took a breather, taking in the photographic beauty around us.

Amid the calm, the loudest noise—not loud at all—came from a squirrel scurrying about in a nearby loblolly pine. Off in the distance, a woodpecker drilled against the wood with the grassy plain chiming in, rustling in a twirly breeze. All these sounds strung together, making nature's music. It was better than any song I'd heard, and I emphatically love music. I could sense we were deep into this reserve. Maybe in the heart of it.

I did allow my mind to imagine that if this type of woodland once more stretched unimpeded throughout the eastern Carolinas, it would be beneficial for the Earth. It would give the endangered red wolf a larger range, along with a host of other animals. In a split second, I thought, it's true that the world could heal its ecosystems if we lost half the human population, freeing up more land for conservation. But I knew I couldn't join forces with Dust. Not just because my daughter was now her opposition, but because I believed humanity, on its own, was already heading in the right direction with the environment.

As far as population control goes, I know that several countries are losing people by natural decline, places where deaths were outnumbering births. This lower birth rate is spreading across the globe due to a confluence of modern trends. Even so, at current rates, it will take time to stabilize or decrease the population. *Have we run out of time?* I'm inclined to believe that more people equals more minds, and with more minds, we can find solutions.

I remembered, despite plenty of negative media reports, that gains are being made on the environment front. I had researched this issue for over twenty years because the environment had always been a passion of mine. I had combed the internet for the positive along with the negative stories. And I had to say that, these days, the positive was beginning to outweigh the negative, although you have to look for it. Was it Mother Nature giving us that tilt in the right direction? It didn't seem like the pro-environment governments, corporations, organizations, and individuals I'd read about were influenced by the Mother Nature world I'd been introduced to this weekend. I hoped they had free will. The idea that our minds were being manipulated by either good or evil nature didn't compute well with me. It was like we were puppets.

Then from the heavens, a wind blew down and formed a tunnel beside us, a portal just like we had walked through earlier. Again, we were being guided by Lily, but I wasn't certain where.

I looked over at an awestruck Logan and said, "That's Lily. We must walk the tunnel."

"Where does it lead?" he asked.

"Either to Tabitha and Rose, the house, or somewhere else entirely."

"OK, let's go." He sounded relieved.

I understood his relief. Lily had made the tough decision for us. She was giving us a path forward. Logan and I stepped inside the wind tunnel and started down Lily's road. I watched his amazement at the whole thing; the two walls of flying debris lined up to our left and right. He reached out to touch.

I yelled, "No! Logan, don't."

He snatched back his fingers, streaked with red. As I feared, they had been sliced by the wall of wind. He brought them to his lips, sucking the hurt or the blood away. "Fuck! That hurt!"

"Let me see." I surveyed the wound. The wall had peeled the skin off two of his fingers, exposing a red layer. He didn't bleed. He was OK. But this had warned us that the two wind-driven walls weren't something to stumble into. That unnerved me as they were gusting only a few feet away on either side.

Logan's demeanor told me he held the same uneasy feeling. We refocused and stayed close to the path's center. A trip on a tree root could send us face-first into that blade-like wall. I locked arms with him, and we carefully walked in step, steadying each other against the deadly torrent at our sides. Claustrophobia seized me briefly, but I managed to shake it off. I zoned in on the woodlands ahead, watching the daylight slowly dissipate as this awful Sunday drew to a close—the beginning of the end.

The longer I walked, the more at ease I grew. But the pervasive thought that I needed to kill all the parents waiting at the old house entered my head again. I turned to prayer to erase it from my mind, but it kept seeping through until it had a stranglehold. I began methodically planning how I would do it, how I would kill them all. *They need to be eliminated,* I tried to convince myself. *They pose too great a risk to the world.*

Logan and I stepped from the wind tunnel's end, where we saw the decaying old plantation house. Night had fully fallen. *Lily wanted us to come back to the house,* I realized. *But she was far from my mind. Too far.* Small lights flickered in the downstairs windows; I assumed they had found candles. No one waited on the porch. Everyone was inside, with Tyler as their only gatekeeper. I grinned, feeling too much excitement at my next mission. Tonight, I had decided, I was going to isolate each of them in turn, on the pretense of questioning them about their involvement with Saris.

In actuality, I intended to kill each of them one by one, except Logan and Tyler. They were the only ones I could trust.

Then Logan started coughing.

My heart sank.

The virus.

CHAPTER 28
The Officer

Officer Blake didn't know what to make of the strange crime scene at Evergreen Baptist Church, unlike any he'd ever investigated. Certainly, crimes had been committed. But he couldn't get the phrase "Act of God" out of his mind, either. Was it God? Or Mother Nature? Whichever, something powerful had intervened after something had gone badly awry with the humans. The air was thick with transgression. Supernatural or not.

Thus far, three dead bodies were discovered. One had been thrown from a tornado, but the other two died from gunshot wounds. One semi-catatonic woman and seven children were the only witnesses to the entire ordeal. Others, who had been chased out of the church by a frightening couple, half-dressed, bloody and brandishing a gun, had only fragmentary evidence to offer. And all of the witness statements baffled Officer Blake. They made nature out to be the real enemy. First, an unnaturally aggressive swarm of bats, out in the daylight, and then a twister. Coincidence?

The parishioners he'd found milling about in the parking lot reported a man and woman barging into the sanctuary armed with a pistol and silencer, ordering them to leave. They had obeyed, dashing away, leaving behind the fourteen who were now reported as missing.

After finishing his interviews, Blake left the scene, expecting the drones and the search parties to find more clues and the missing people, alive or not. He acted on a hunch by driving down the road that led into that new subdivision behind the church. His best friend lived back there. *Tyler.* The description of the bloody, armed couple sounded disturbingly like Tyler and his wife, Misty. Throughout the morning, Blake sent a series of unanswered texts and two phone calls to Tyler. The long silence was uncharacteristic. They were friends who kept in touch.

As Blake wheeled his patrol car around a bend in the subdivision's main street, a fallen tree forced him to stomp on the brakes, screeching to a stop, rubber burning into the pavement. The tree lay directly across the street, like a blockade to Tyler's house. As he stepped out of the vehicle, a spooky feeling inundated him. The wind blew around him in a bone-chilling twist, and the air had a faint smell of embers.

Even more compelled to investigate, Blake left the patrol car, picked his way around the fallen tree, and headed to Tyler's house on foot. He recalled how his relationship with Tyler had been tested four years ago, the fateful evening when Amelia Smith died under Tyler's custody. The woman had collapsed at the police station's doors. After EMTs raced her to the hospital, she was declared dead on arrival.

A few days afterward, Tyler had confessed to Blake that he had violated departmental protocol when arresting her. He'd admitted that he was mad at the world that night, and had declared a solitary war on drugs. He'd been sick of the overdoses, and the families and communities torn apart by opioids. Tyler confided to Blake that he'd manhandled Amelia into handcuffs and into the patrol car, hurting her, and that he hadn't taken her in right away. Instead, he'd driven her around, looking for her dealer to arrest, while Amelia cried out in pain. It still chilled Blake to remember how Tyler quoted Amelia's screams: "You broke my arm, you son of a bitch. I need to go to the hospital! Take me there now!"

He'd ignored her pleas, Tyler had admitted.

When Blake asked why he hadn't taken her straight to the hospital, Tyler answered, "I thought she was acting, trying to con me into taking her to the E.R. You know; to get morphine or some other narcotic, pain meds. Something for the withdrawals she was going through."

Blake had believed him. He remembered that the coroner's report said she had had a heart attack due to years of constant drug use. Nothing was written about a broken arm or any other injury. But Tyler's admission of roughhousing Amelia had never sat well. As a police officer, Blake firmly believed, you have to keep the utmost control of your emotions.

As an African American himself, Blake would have defended his friend from charge of racism if it had come to that. He told himself this wasn't because they were friends but because Blake could read someone's intent and nature. It was a skill he had honed over nineteen years as a police officer. That's why Blake never reported what Tyler told him. Besides, Tyler had an impeccable record in law enforcement.

Despite that record, however, Blake wouldn't have defended his friend from a charge of unprofessional behavior. He thought Tyler had deserved some kind of suspension or time out, but nothing happened because if Blake had reported him, that would put Tyler squarely in a shit-storm due to the nation's sensitivities. There would have been no middle ground of punishment for Tyler. Instead, the incident hadn't become a national scandal; it hadn't even made the local news. And, after all, Amelia Smith had been high on heroin. The only "contributing factor" for her heart attack had been recorded as an overdose, an all too common way to die during the past decade. As he walked toward Tyler's house, Blake kept returning to that memory. His cop instincts told him that the Amelia Smith incident was somehow tied to today.

During that morning's investigation, Blake had found out that Tyler lived on the same street as Evergreen Church's dead pastor, Saris. Who had been Amelia's husband. He guessed Tyler had been unaware of a least one of those facts, or at least until this weekend. It seemed Saris had known exactly who Tyler was and that he had devised a long-game plot to get revenge. But it appeared that Saris's plan had fallen apart. He had been found dead, at his own church. Or—the thought kept nagging at Blake—had he wanted to die?

About to round a blind curve that led to Tyler's house, Blake smelled something smoldering. He charged around a patch of woods to see nothing but a teepee of charred lumber where the house had stood. The mystery grew more complex and bewildering when Blake noticed a black trail of scorched earth curving off the street—like gasoline had been poured along the pavement. Another bend in the street hid the far end of that scorched strip, but Blake knew Saris's house was down there. Even before he got close enough to see, he had a pretty good idea that it had burned up, as well.

So many scenarios of what had gone down scrolled through Blake's mind as he searched Tyler's property for clues. He wouldn't have been surprised if he'd come upon yet another corpse. The undeveloped land remained unsettlingly quiet all around him. Blake wasn't one for nature walks. He wasn't accustomed to being this far away from people. He wasn't sure why, but something kept making him look over his shoulder. But he never saw anything. And after completing a full circle search around the charred ruins, he didn't find any corpse. Yet. He didn't dive into the burnt heap of Tyler's house, though. This would require forensics experts, arson investigators. Blake knew better than to tamper with potential evidence.

He then set his sights on the charred path toward Saris's house, but he decided to call this in and ask for backup before continuing. Blake didn't want to admit it to himself yet, but he was afraid. It was a strange feeling for him; he didn't live his life in fear. Being a police officer, he'd grown numb to that inconvenient emotion.

He pulled out his phone, and the screen was blank. Blake pushed the power-on button, and nothing happened. A dead battery? He became unsettled being cut off from communication and civilization. A long hike separated him from his patrol car and its radio to the world. Suspicion washed over him. He remembered distinctly having a fully charged phone before leaving the church just minutes ago. After a second thought, he concluded paranoia was at play; there was no way someone could have messed with his phone and drained the battery.

At that instant, Blake felt eyes upon him. He spun around to see a woman who had seemingly appeared out of nowhere. She was gorgeous, with long black hair falling to her waist, framing a voluptuous figure. "Captivated" was not precisely the word to describe Blake's reaction at seeing her. He was more ensnared by her womanly magnetism. The femininity that emanated from her meshed all too perfectly with his masculine urges. The scent that wafted from her body touched Blake, in a deep-rooted, ancestral appeal.

In the depths of his mind, he struggled to return to the image of the wife he loved dearly, who had always been in the forefront of his mind—until now. This new female presence pushed Blake's wife deep into his soul's deepest, most cavernous recesses. Just when Blake tried to remember that he was happily married, this woman dealt him a new blow, unleashing the power of her voice.

"Hello, there. I'm Dusty." Her voice stroked him, or felt like she did.

He was hard. Harder than he'd ever been. Dusty's light brown dress was sheer enough that he could make out everything. She wore no garment underneath, showing her true curvature and her true intention—which was to fuck. Her full flesh on display reminded Blake of a renaissance painting, except that this woman wasn't Caucasian, but of Native American heritage. But like that classic nude, Dusty's ample body was more toned.

He felt like the woman before him belonged to that distant time. Like centuries hadn't passed. Blake didn't respond to her greeting. He couldn't. His lips hung apart. He couldn't move them to form words. So he listened again to her stroking vocals.

"Follow me . . ."

Dusty sauntered off the road and into the woods. Blake followed the gravitational pull into her sensual aura. She hadn't gotten far before she stopped, turned, and held her hand out.

Transfixed, Blake halted.

Provocatively, Dusty bent her shoulders together, allowing her see-through dress to droop enough to fall off. The garment formed a ring at her feet, instantly metamorphosing into a brown snake that slithered away. She stepped closer to Blake.

The curves of her body ran smoothly, culminating in high breasts that pointed upward, drawing the hapless officer toward them, his lips parted and hungry. While he rolled his mouth down to her navel and then below, Dusty swiftly undressed Blake, every seductive motion part of a relentless flow. He buried his face into the triangle of short black hair where her long legs joined. His tongue marked the orifice that would be his to conquer. Dusty met the officer's attentions with approval, sending him signals that she found him attractive, that she desired him like any mortal woman would.

He sat up, and their lips met ravenously. Blake tasted something wild as they probed each other in an immersive kiss. Both of them entirely nude in the sun-drenched forest, she glided her bare body against his, her caresses raising goose-pimples wherever her smooth skin touched his. In one swift movement, he placed himself inside her, stimulating him into oblivion more than any pharmaceutical could. Her manner, suggesting she had relinquished control, reassured Blake that Dusty was submitting wholly to him—a middle-aged man, to be sure, but one who knew what he was doing.

Any sexual fantasy he'd ever had since adolescence—it was torn asunder by her. By the glory of having her. His imagination couldn't erect this level of fantasy, because even imaginations have flaws, and all of her was flawless. She invoked the dormant man underneath, bringing out the stoic masculinity that hulked through him like a celebratory fire; embers from his glorious blaze touched the stratosphere.

He resolved that he would gladly fight the strongest man in the world to prove his machismo to this sinfully sexy woman. Blake shared the same instinct that an American bighorn ram has for dominance, head-butting its rivals. He imagined hearing their horns clashing on a mountainside somewhere in the western United States. The image drummed up Blake's male hormones, and with each imagined clash, he rammed Dusty. He took short deep breaths, inhaling the combined essence of her and the sweet blooming fauna, but they were one and the same. Dusty was all of nature's beauty; all that he wanted her to be.

Above them, a red-tailed hawk flew through the yellow pollen that drifted in the light, curling up the plant dust in its wake like an airplane bursting through the clouds. No allergies, no ailments here, only nature's most natural act. Under the sun's heavenly shine, and in between two giant pine trees, that act continued with their bodies rippling in rapid concert with every joining of flesh.

Blake, fully induced by a feverish dose of Dusty's sexuality, could feel the sudden rush of his seed, ready to burst out. And suddenly, he froze inside her to keep the explosion one match's touch away. Any slight vibration would finish him.

Then he felt Dusty carefully dislodging herself from him. She seemed to know that Blake was a landmine. After all, she had built and planted it. Dusty pulling away signified that she didn't want to be done either. "Nice to meet you," she said with a playful giggle.

The officer still couldn't talk. This high, this bliss, this whatever this was, had rendered him mute. Once separated from her sweet embrace, he immediately and impatiently wanted to rejoin her. To feel those warm fluids smack against his erection, that hot friction. *Enough with the self-denying prolonging,* Blake thought, as if to present his demand to her.

Not letting a second more go by, his mouth went down upon her neck in a nibbling bite that resolved into a tongue-filled battle against her skin. Blake insinuated himself inside her again, finding even more wetness this time.

Dusty gasped, confirming in his mind the value of the pleasure he so aggressively bestowed upon her. "Three hundred years," she murmured between breaths. "No mortal man—until now," she rasped in his ear.

Her nails clawed into his broad back.

It's not that she was playing rough, he guessed, from the pre-orgasm way her body clenched. No, his ego was pleased to conclude, this act provided an outlet from the immense pleasure gushing through her, all the result of his skillful motions. The wet smacking they created picked up speed.

Dusty demanded, "Giiiiive iiiiit toooo meeeeee nowwwww."

All good sensations in Blake's life coalesced toward his groin. The catatonic euphoria he felt reached its zenith . . . and he spurted his warm life into Dusty. Both screamed final cries of release, frightening any of nature's small creatures within earshot. The sun glowed upon them in their afterglow. Sweat shimmered on their bodies. Blake was drained. Completely drained. He couldn't move, wrapped firmly in Dusty's arms. She held him tight, as if he was exactly where she wanted him. Like she would never let him go.

Languidly, Dusty murmured into his ear. "Officer, I spotted two girls lost in these woods. They need to be found and rescued. Brought back into the world. They may resist, but I know you will do your job."

He reveled in the sweet, hypnotic tones of her voice. For the first time, Blake spoke to her. "I will find them and bring them home." He said this soldier-like, snapping his nude body to attention, still firmly within her grasp.

Dusty slid her fingers along his bare shoulder. "Their names are Tabitha and Rose," she said, resuming her most seductive tone. "Now you have to go and find them. My wonderful, delectable man." Blake reveled in the feeling as Dusty gave his ass a last firm squeeze. Opening his eyes, he caught her most beguiling smile. Then, in the blink of an eye, she disappeared.

Blake, left alone and bare, found his clothes in a heap next to him. Perplexed and vaguely ashamed, he didn't know what to think about what had just happened—did it happen?—but knew he had a mission to perform. Once he had buttoned himself back into his uniform, he looked around, confirmed that he was utterly alone, and stepped resolutely forward into the forest.

The hunt was on.

He had to find Tabitha and Rose.

CHAPTER 29

Three Widowed Men

Somebody's coughing knocked my malicious plans from my mind. I wasn't sure if it was Lily's, or Logan's. I regained myself, or at least I hoped I had. I had just convinced myself that killing everyone was the best path forward. Not only did I have to worry about the parents breaking quarantine, I also had to watch myself. I wasn't as impervious to Dust's influence as I'd thought. I had lost my logic, my self-awareness. I needed to go into this strange old house and tell Tyler as soon as possible so he could be on the lookout for anything different in me.

Logan wheezed out the last in a machine-gun flurry of coughing before joining me in a run toward the house. I turned a rusty knob, and opened the door into a room—holding nobody. Candles burned on various ancient furniture in corners, and everything was clean and polished, as if people lived here. But the house was too quiet. Not a sound came from upstairs.

Then she stepped out in front of me. Dust looked different. She was in human form, which frightened me more than her devilish appearances before. She wore a long, provocative gown and carried a confidence I'd never seen before.

I turned to Logan and commanded, "Don't look at her."

He already had his head turned toward the door. He knew the lure of her ways all too well. I expected him to run out at any moment. I could feel the heat of Dusty's glare upon my cheek, challenging me to face her. I easily lost; my gaze was drawn into her eyes.

Her silky voice oozed from between pouty lips. "Misty, you should join me."

"Never," I retorted. But then I had to ask, "Where is everybody?"

Dusty rolled her eyes. "They're fine. Unfortunately." She stared at me for a long moment.

"Don't worry. I'm done trying to get into your mind. I simply can't. You've done nothing but fight me off before coming in here. I am trying to sell you on something. Since I can't do that in my usual way, let me just say: contrary to what your daughter says, evil is actually necessary. Without it, think about the world that it leaves. Everyone living in harmony sounds good on paper, but what if that actually happened? The dullness of no conflict of any kind would eventually whittle humanity back into an animal that lives on pure instinct. Your self-awareness would turn to *dust*. The duality that's around you keeps you sharp. Think about it."

Then, in the snap of a finger, Dust turned to dust. The house creaked, and the walls around us suddenly aged, as if a century had passed in a second.

Logan turned back, and we both watched in awe as the house withered into the state it is in today. I didn't realize when we first entered that we had walked into another time. I remembered my dream with Mist; the woods had looked different, and as she explained, it was because we were in the 1500s.

When the house had filled with cobwebs, dust and mold, it stopped creaking. The aging ceased. Out of thin air, I half saw Tyler appear before me. My shoulders were being jerked back and forth. He was shouting, "Misty, are you there?"

I dived into him. I felt all of him there. Ever so thankful that he was alive, I leaped to his lips and kissed the man that I loved—more than loved.

He reciprocated briefly and gently pushed me away. "Misty, what happened?" he asked. "You were in a trance. I couldn't wake you. Logan was the same way."

I answered, "When we walked into this house, we entered a different time. Dust was there in her human form, and she tried to recruit me to follow her instead of Lily." I lowered my voice to a whisper, noticing the parents sitting around us. "Tyler, you have to watch me, because she did get into my mind. I had an evil thought that was hard to shake. I was merciless; I wanted to kill everyone here. Not because it was right, but because it offered an easier path to victory."

Tyler looked perplexed by my admission. He shuffled me toward a corner away from everyone. Softly, he said, "If you wanted to kill everyone here, then that victory would belong to Lily."

A lightbulb went off inside me. He was right. How would it benefit Dust's goal, *which is to infect humanity*, if I killed everyone who was infected? Dust had just said that mentally I fought her off successfully; maybe it was an unconscious battle that my conscious mind couldn't register as having won.

Now I wondered if it had been Lily who got into my mind when we were on the wind-tunnel path. Did she want me to kill everyone here, except Tyler and Logan, because they'd been spared from my possessed mind? Killing people seemed to belong to the evil nature—unless these parents are evil, not worth saving. Like Kelly, for one. They all have kids; but does that exempt them from death? To save humankind, would they have to go, even before the virus killed them?

Lily had told me none of those left worked for Saris, but at any moment any of them could still be influenced by Dust. Suddenly, I had to know: who are these parents? Where did they stand mentally at all times?

Should they live?

Tyler watched me piece together his statement, and he seemed to wait for me to give him an order. *An order to kill.* I scoped the room, where ten parents sat in flickering shadows.

Kelly's husband, Daniel, stood out to me first. He sat up and impatiently asked what I expected him to ask. "Where's my wife? Did you find my daughters?"

Logan, who hadn't moved from the door, showed an uneasy shift in his posture at Tabitha's father's question.

I answered, somewhat coldly, to rip the bandage off, "We couldn't find your daughters," I said bluntly. Without pausing, I went on, "And your wife was working with Saris. So we killed her."

I expected a ferocious burst from this man. Because I did kill his wife. But he calmly sat back down. "I knew it all along. I even caught them once having sex. In our house. I went back outside and pretended I never saw it." He shook his head. "If I confronted the affair, then divorce would be inevitable, and I couldn't do that to our daughters. As clichéd as it sounds, I stayed for the kids. But something else changed in my wife; a coldness that wasn't there before. Was that Dust? Is that why you killed her—?" He choked on the last sentence, holding back tears.

I answered more softly, "Yes, I had to do it. As I explained earlier, there's a virus running through you. It has the capacity to wipe out half the world's population. This was planned and executed by Saris. And by your wife, Kelly."

Sitting next to Daniel sat Becky's grief-stricken husband. *Another man who just lost his wife.* I addressed him directly. "And I assume your wife Becky worked with them as well. She raced to open the room that was full of bats …"

Becky's husband didn't acknowledge me, but his face reflected an understanding.

I remembered that a third widowed man sat among these parents. His wife had been tossed by the tornado; her motionless eyes had sent a chilling shiver through me.

Before I could say anything to him, someone knocked on the front door. Logan, just inches away, jumped. I could hear hearts pounding, from fear or excitement.

The tide was about to change.

Chapter 30

Kindred Spirits

With me standing close behind him, Logan cautiously twisted the knob, and the weathered door opened. Immense release in his voice, he stammered, "Tabitha. You're alive."

Timidly, she stepped back, revealing her little sister curled around her leg. From behind them, a uniformed police officer came forward, and I instantly recognized him. I turned to Tyler, swelling with relief, and said, "Hon, your best friend, Blake, is here."

I loved Blake in a big brother way. He was part of the family.

Daniel zipped past me to hug his girls, Tabitha and Rose, whom he'd feared were lost forever.

I hugged Blake, and Tyler did so after me.

Oddly, I got a sense of remorse from Blake. I scanned the porch and the overgrown yard behind him for any of his fellow officers but didn't see anyone else. *Thank God,* I thought. We can't allow the press—the world—to come flooding upon this house. I wouldn't have known how to stop the virus from spreading if that occurred.

"Bro, do you know why we're here?" Tyler asked.

"I'm not sure," Blake answered, "A strange woman lured me into—" Blake cut himself off and looked down, shamefaced.

I said, bluntly, "Her name is Dust. And that wasn't a mortal woman."

Blake looked at me, no sign of surprise in his eyes. He seemed to know he had encountered something beyond a normal human.

Tyler said, "Bro, a lot has happened since we talked last. The world as you know it is about to change."

I stepped back while my husband caught Blake up. I listened in as Tabitha, beside me, told her dad about seeing her mom before she died. My stomach curdled; I hadn't known I'd left Kelly alive long enough to tell her daughters good bye. I thought I'd killed her point-blank. I certainly hadn't wanted those girls to see their mother like that. But I remembered that Kelly was the enemy, and had almost killed Logan.

He just hid away in a corner. I assumed he didn't want to look at Tabitha, out of shame for what he'd done.

Despite the dust and the gloom, the ancient room had a family reunion, get-together feel. Except that it wasn't. Without warning, the front door behind Daniel and his daughters slammed shut. At first, I thought it was the wind. But then the old house lit up. In every room, a bright light appeared against the ceiling. Time shuddered. Everyone froze, and in the light I could see their faces clearly. In their eyes I could see the hurt, the loneliness, the apprehension, the guilt, and the fear of the unknown.

Tyler was frozen in place.

I was the only one who moved.

"Mom," Lily's voice came out of nowhere.

"Lily?" I couldn't see her but felt her heavenly presence.

She spoke directly to me. "I never wanted you to kill these parents. That was Dust. All of the people in this house right now are innocent. I'm going to send you all to the past to quarantine. I was just waiting for everyone infected to unite here. You will remain in the past for thirty days until the virus leaves your systems. The time that I'm sending you to will negate the virus. That means nobody will die from the virus, but the environment will be harsh, especially to people alive in the twenty-first century. People could still die from other perils. You'll still be in North Carolina but 15,000 years earlier. Watch out for smilodons; they look like a saber-toothed cat. Be on the lookout for any other predatory animals that are extinct today. And of course all the familiar predators that are still around. That long ago, they were far more powerful. Finding food and water will be the easy part. Shelter and surviving the elements will be more difficult."

With an upbeat shift in her speech, Lily added. "But Mom, you can let the world's weight go."

I couldn't say anything except, "We're going to be in a different time for thirty days?"

Lily reaffirmed this. "Yes, Mom. Staying here in the present will be too dangerous. If you did, at least half of you would die. The risk to the world is too great. Going back in time, you will have a better chance. Humanity will have a better chance. Find that inner instinct in you to survive. Dig deep." With that, Lily's presence left me again.

I couldn't believe we were going to be sent thousands of years into the past. *This can't be our only option*, I thought.

The room came back to life, everyone was animate again, and once again, candles were the only light.

I screamed. "Everybody listen! Lily is sending us back in time." Just as my warning came out, and before anyone could process what I'd said, the house shook. The walls folded back and seemed to dissolve, exposing us to the outside. The night woods moved as trees changed, weirdly changing, some growing taller and others shorter. Shooting stars streamed across the sky like constantly exploding fireworks stretched across the globe. Behind the streaks of light, only the moon seemed to stay steady. Then the time-shifting stopped. The cold struck my bones, and snow pocketed the ground. The trees were more evergreen, but the longleaf pines were gone. These new ones, or rather old ones, were cone-shaped, rising tall like Christmas trees for giants.

I reached out for Tyler's hand. Our breath was visible in the frigid air. He curled his hand around mine and held it tight.

"Together," he whispered.

We had yet another fight ahead of us. But this time, it was about sheer survival against the elements. Not a modern-day version of survival. Or maybe, at its core, it was no different. Whether you're thriving financially based on your own merit or by someone else's hard work: if you take the money out of it, people are still divided the same way. Either you contribute or you don't. There are many ways someone could contribute, and that contribution will be necessary for us to survive. Laziness in its many forms will not persist in the untamed world we were standing on.

Sixteen people, counting myself, stood in this chilly clearing in the boreal forest. In thirty days, would sixteen be left? If we stuck together, used our heads, and each pulled our weight, then we could all still be here in a month. I read once that a person who lived thirty-five years during this ancient era would be far more intelligent than someone of the same age in our century, simply because it would have taken a brilliant human to survive nature for that long. The obstacles were not as rudimentary as one might think. People might think it took athleticism to survive 13,000 B.C.

Oh, it's so much more than that. I was about to find out what it truly took to make it through this time.

End of Book One

I grew up with an active imagination. I'm a child of the '90s who had few distractions like the world has today, like smartphones, Netflix, etc. So in my free time, I created my own stories and games. Often the stories would be in my head, not written down. At bedtime, if I had trouble falling asleep right away, I would daydream my stories to life. I'd put myself into a character and sometimes spend hours mapping out the plot. Each night I would pick up where I left off; this would help me sleep. Before long, a catalog of different stories existed in my daydreams; Netflix for the mind, so to speak. With this book, I decided to finally put pen to paper—or keystrokes to computer.